You Are Dead.
(Sign Here Please)

by Andrew Stanek

Sign up for my mailing list at http://eepurl.com/bhTc9H to receive emails from me about my writing, including information about sales and book giveaways!

--Andrew Stanek

Prologue

One of the most inexplicably peculiar things about humans is their enduring fear of death. Death numbers among the greatest fears that humans have. It isn't number one but ranks a strong number five or six, just after public speaking, spiders, heights, clowns, and forgetting to put your clothes on before going outside. This is peculiar because, rationally speaking, since no one has ever died before, no one knows what will happen afterward, and therefore you should make no assumptions whatsoever about it, including assuming that it might be unpleasant or in any way worse than life. But humans continue to fly in the face of rational judgment by fearing death, thereby assuming that death is a bad experience, even though colossally huge numbers of people mope around complaining about how horrible their lives are, while almost everyone who has ever died has elected to stay dead rather than come back to life and complain about their death experiences. Those who have chosen to come back to life tend to have done so an immensely long time ago, suggesting that if the afterlife was in any way unpleasant previously, it has remarkably improved over time, while life itself has - if the mopers are to be believed - remained a lengthy marathon of toil and drudgery, with only shiny gadgets and reality TV to distract us from our unpleasant existences.

Because most people who have ever lived have died, those that haven't are left with a strong suspicion that they are next and the end might be coming for them any day now. Therefore, most major world religions have developed their own beliefs about the afterlife. Christians, for example, believe that after death the righteous are sent to bask in eternal bliss in the light of god while the wicked burn in endless torture in hell (which probably tells you something about the people who fear death). Hindus believe that after death your soul is recycled back into the world and you are reincarnated into a better existence if you had good karma and a worse existence if you had bad karma - which means - as with the Christians - fear of death is predicated entirely on the suspicion that you might have done something horribly unforgivable in your present life. Buddhists also believe in reincarnation, although the Dalai Lama, a prominent Buddhist spiritual leader, recently floated the suggestion that he thought he'd had a pretty good run this time and he might not reincarnate after all. There has as yet been no word from him about what he intends to spend eternity doing if not reincarnating into infinite mortal iterations of himself.

So everyone has their own theory about what happens. The Christians believe in heaven and hell. The Hindus believe in reincarnation. Horace Pickelfern of 289 Timbercrest Road, Anchorage, believes that after death everyone is hugged by a giant spirit bear, and if you fail to hug him back then he mauls you to double-death and you have to progress to the after-after-life, which is on the whole less pleasant. But the one thing that they all agree on - even Horace Pickelfern - is that when you die you finally get answers. Whether in heaven or hell, you get to sit down with your creator (or his designated proxy) and have a nice long chat about the meaning of life, at which point you presumably learn the meaning of your particular life and if you did it right.

As a certain Mr. Nathan Haynes of Nevada was about to find out, they were all wrong.

Chapter 1

"Hello. I'm here to kill you."

Nathan blinked.

"What?" he asked.

The man standing on the doorstep smiled broadly.

"Hello," he repeated. He reached out and seized Nathan's palms in a jaunty handshake. "I'm here to kill you."

Nathan blinked again. There was a pause.

"Oh yes, yes of course!" he exclaimed. "Do come in." Nathan stood aside and the smiling man walked briskly into his foyer. He looked around and smiled at the modest furnishings.

"You have a very lovely home."

"Thank you for saying so - Mr. - er, what did you say your name was again?"

The man's smile broadened even further.

"I'd rather not say."

"I understand completely," Nathan said, his voice thick with sympathy. "You can't be too careful - so many weirdos around. Now, you said you were here to kill me?"

"That's right."

"How very interesting! Please have a seat." Nathan waved him into a nearby comfy chair.

"Oh, I couldn't possibly impose-"

"Sit - sit," Nathan insisted. "Make yourself comfortable."

"Well, if you insist."

The smiling man sank down into the greenest of Nathan's several green chairs. Nathan took the opposite chair.

"Can I offer you anything?"

"Oh, no, thank you very much. I'm fine."

"I remember you called ahead," Nathan said, frowning.

"I'm afraid I can't quite remember what you said - I have a medical condition, you see -"

"-I had heard about that, yes-"

"-but I remember you said that it was terribly important that you kill me-"

"-yes, exactly, extremely urgent."

"Why was that again?"

"Ah, that's getting straight to the heart of the matter." The smiling man rubbed his hands together. "Very direct. I like it. You see, I am a serial killer."

"Are you *really*?" Nathan said with astonishment. "How does one get to be a serial killer?"

"It's mainly a matter of personal choice and, if you don't mind my saying, willpower."

"How interesting."

"Yes - well, as a serial killer, it is my job - and I would go so far as to say my duty - to murder as many people as possible."

"Of course, of course, that makes perfect sense," Nathan said fervently. "I don't suppose it could be any other way, could it?"

"No indeed. But I have a problem. I haven't killed anyone in a fair long while."

"Really? Why is that?"

"It's sad to say, but one encounters rather a lot of negativity as a serial killer. It's all 'no, please don't!' and 'you're an awful person' and 'stop in the name of the law, this is the police, we have you totally surrounded, come out with your hands up.' And well, with all of it, I just fell into a bit of a rut, and it's been a while since I've killed anyone at all, and that's not good for business. Just between you and me, I shouldn't have let it go quite this long - embarrassing really - but I just sort of woke up this morning and realized that the papers were all full of reports about other serial killers and none about me at all! So, you see, it's extremely important that I murder someone right away. Otherwise I'll fall behind the Gunderland Strangler and the Oregon Truck Stop Killer, and we can't have that, can we?"

"No, no, of course not," responded Nathan, who was obviously supposed to agree. "I understand completely that you're in something of a bind, but why do you need to kill me particularly?"

"I'm happy you mentioned that. I received an excellent tip that you have an unusual medical condition."

"That's right. I have - um - a sort of brain lesion and a condition. It's actually a bit like an amnesia. It makes it hard to remember things sometimes. I remember it had something to do with my hippocampus... either I have too much hippocampus or not enough hippocampus or the right amount but in the wrong place or something, but the point is that I have brain damage, and it's left me with no self preservation instinct whatsoever."

"Really? None at all."

"No, none at all."

"Yes, well you must see that's absolutely perfect for me," the smiling man continued. He thrust out his wrist and checked his watch. "But I don't think I have to kill you quite yet if I want to make the evening news, so we have a few minutes to talk. And color me intrigued. You mean you don't have any self-interest at all? You don't care what happens to you?"

"Oh no, that's not it at all," Nathan said, shaking his head. "I care quite a lot about what happens to me. I get very mad if I can't get my morning cup of coffee or if my neighbors are too loud and keep me up and night. It's just that I have no fear of death."

"How extraordinary! And can you tell right from wrong? Good from evil?"

"Er - I have a little more trouble with that," Nathan admitted. "I guess that's just a consequence of the brain damage. My doctors told me that I needed to be very careful because my condition would make me very suggestible to people who would want to take advantage of me - present company excluded, of course. I don't think I have anything to fear from an honest, upstanding serial killer such as yourself."

"Is there anything that makes you suspicious?"

"Suspicious? Oh yes. I'm suspicious all the time. I remember I was watching a report on the news just the other night about a con artist who was tricking people into signing over their houses to him. I'm always careful about signing things - I think with all this fine print and legalese these days, you never know exactly what you're agreeing to."

"I agree completely."

"You don't need me to sign anything, do you?" Nathan asked anxiously.

"No, nothing."

"Oh, that's good." Relief was palpable in Nathan's voice. "So you can kill me without any paperwork at all?"

"Yes! I conduct completely paperless murders. In fact, I view a paper trail as something of a detriment. It could cause complications further down the road."

"With litigation, you mean?"

"Yes. Something like that."

"I like your attitude," Nathan said fervently. "If more small businessmen had ideas like yours, the world would be a better place. I remember not so long ago I was listening to something about murders on the news. I think it was how we don't have nearly enough murders. Yes, that must have been it."

The serial killer's smile broadened. He checked his watch again.

"Well, I think it's just about time," he said. "You do live alone, don't you?"

"Oh yes. Totally alone."

"Good, good." As he spoke, the serial killer was drawing the blinds on all of Nathan's windows. "And do you have a cell phone or a webcam or cameras or anything like that?"

"No. I don't hold with most of this modern technology. I don't even have a computer."

"Really? None at all?"

"I did have a laptop but it's broken now," Nathan admitted. "But I never quite got the hang of using it to begin with."

"So no cell phone or cameras - excellent. And do you have a land line?"

"Yes, right over there." Nathan pointed to his phone, which sat on the wall of his living room.

"We'll just have to take care of that," the smiling man said cheerily. He walked over to it, reached into his pocket, and took out a small pair of wire cutters, then snipped the phone line.

"Hey!" Nathan exclaimed, jumping to his feet. "Was that entirely necessary?"

"Yes, I'm afraid so," the man said apologetically. "I'm very sorry for any inconvenience I've caused you, but we're almost done. Just one last question - would you say this room is soundproof?"

"Oh, no, not at all. The neighbors are awfully loud.

Sometimes they keep me up all night."

"I see. We'll need this, then. Where did I put that?" The smiling man rummaged through his pockets, patting himself down until he found a long metal tube covered with honeycombed structures - a silencer, Nathan realized. The man then produced a semiautomatic pistol and screwed the silencer into the barrel.

"Now, could you just look over there for me?"

Nathan obediently looked at the indicated point on his own wall.

"Some people prefer to close their eyes," the smiling man added. "This won't hurt a bit."

Nathan felt the cold, metal tip of the gun's barrel in the back of his head. Then there was a muffled bang and the world went black.

Chapter 2

The whole world was infinite unending blackness. Then, through the vast nothing, Nathan heard a mechanical woman's voice. It sounded like a loudspeaker.

"Station number four, please."

As the voice spoke, a little desk jumped into existence directly in front of Nathan. The desk was large and square, stacked high with files, with a little snowglobe-paperweight sitting on top of the highest one. Behind the desk there was a slightly unattractive frumpy-looking woman wearing a heavy sweater and blocky glasses. Her expression was severe, her face lined, and black bags circled underneath her eyes. Her light hair was done up into a tight bun at the back of her head. She did not look pleased to see him. Nathan was not particularly happy to see her either - her sweater was a strikingly ugly shade of orange.

The woman glanced up at him with distaste, then spoke briskly and tersely.

"You are dead. Sign here please."

She pushed a piece of paper across the desk towards him and gestured towards an adjacent blue china mug full of pens. Nathan plucked out a blue fountain pen that suited him and stared down at the paper she had indicated. It was just one page, but it was covered from top to bottom in the most incredibly dense legalese in a font so unimaginably small that Nathan felt he would have needed something like a scanning electron microscope to decipher the print. At the bottom, the words, "the undersigned agrees to all of the above terms," were visible, considerably larger than all the rest. There were two blanks with the labels "Print Name" and "Signature," underneath.

Nathan felt slightly disoriented and he was about to do as he was told. He took the pen and moved it to the paper. He was just about to sign when he paused, his pen hovering a quarter-inch or so above the page.

He frowned. The memory of the news report about a fraudster who was tricking people into signing over the deeds to their houses dimly flashed through his mind.

He looked up. The frumpy-looking woman was paying him no attention and was instead flipping rapidly through a very heavy file, which was filled with pages just like the one she had pushed towards Nathan. Every so often she made little tutting noises. After a few moments, she turned slightly and noticed Nathan was not signing. She glowered at him.

"Print your name here and sign there," she said. "There's no need to date it. That sort of thing doesn't matter much here."

"What is it?" Nathan asked.

"It's a 21B - Decedent Acknowledgement and Waiver of Liability. It says that you understand that you are dead and that you agree to waive any liability and hold us harmless for any damages - mental, physical, spiritual, or otherwise - that you might incur during your stay in the afterlife. Sign it and hand it back to me so I can countersign. Then you have three more abbreviated waivers to fill out in triplicate, but you only have to initial those. Hurry up about it. There are people in line behind you, you know. We've had almost a hundred new arrivals since you got here."

Nathan frowned down at the densely inked form. He quickly reached a decision.

"I won't sign it."

The woman blinked.

"But you have to sign it."

She looked, if anything, confused, almost as if no one had ever said this before.

Nathan put back the pen and drew away from the table. He crossed his arms, demonstrating that he had absolutely no intention of signing the form.

Now the woman was staring at him with incredulity mixed into the same expression of distaste that she had originally.

"Most irregular," she murmured. "Why won't you sign your 21B?"

"I don't want to," Nathan replied stubbornly. He was not entirely sure why he didn't want to sign the form. It was the principle of the thing, he supposed. On the whole Nathan simply did not hold with form-signing. He made a habit of avoiding it. Nathan very much thought of people who signed forms as types who walked around in suits and chatted to each other about things he found wholly deplorable, like the business news and the weather. Also, the vague suspicion that this was all somehow an incredibly elaborate ruse to steal his house continued to whirl around in the back of his mind. As this was probably the more rational of his concerns, the little voices that ran his brain decided this was the best explanation to vocalize to the woman, who was pointedly waiting for him to say something.

"This could be a trick. You might be trying to steal my house," he said.

The woman's eyebrows shot up into her hair - quite judgmentally, in Nathan's opinion.

"Do you not believe that you're dead?" she asked.

Memories of the sensation of the serial killer's gun pressed against Nathan's temple and the final report of the gunshot before everything had gone black played back through Nathan's head like a film. That nice serial killer had gone to all the trouble of explaining that he was going to kill Nathan and then did exactly what he had promised. Nathan felt a bit stupid. As he didn't like feeling stupid, the voices in his head rapidly devised a new line of defense.

"Well, of course I'm dead," he said matter-of-factly. "But you still might be after my house. Or maybe you're trying to get my clock. I have quite a nice clock."

At this, the woman stared at him with disbelief mixed with utterly palpable hatred.

"I'm afraid I will need to fetch my supervisor," she informed Nathan. "My superiors will have to be informed of this."

She stood and walked to the right. A door appeared out of nothing. She opened it and walked through it. It dissolved into nothing behind her.

Nathan was now left alone in the room, the portions of which that existed were quite small. (The portions that didn't exist were infinite, but Nathan wasn't quite sure he should count those.) He would have liked to sit down, but there was nowhere to sit on his side of the desk. He briefly toyed with the idea that there were no chairs wherever he was, but this idea was smashed to pieces by the fact that there was a chair on the other side of the desk - recently vacated by the frumpy woman. Despite himself, Nathan tutted. The nerve of some people - not even offering a chair to a guest. Well, he assumed he was a guest.

He glanced at the vast array of files that were stacked high on the frumpy woman's desk. For his whole life Nathan had had a slightly nosy streak when it came to other people's desks, and he gathered that a little obstacle like death hadn't put an end to it. While artists and poets liked to insist that art and poetry (respectively) were the window on the soul, in Nathan's experience these things had largely consisted of exhibits of large numbers of brightly colored cardboard boxes and mismatched lines of unfamiliar and annoyingly not-rhyming verse (respectively). The true window on the soul was the desk. What was so personal, so uniquely your own, as your desk? A person's desk was his own place of work - littered with his favorite pens, notebooks, miscellaneous receipts, and occasionally misplaced wallet and passport, while generally his art consisted of nothing more than copies of a few Monets and his poetry the Shakespearean sonnets that he'd been forced to learn in middle school.

So Nathan felt tremendous interest in - and in fact solidarity with - desks. Desks were the only piece of furniture that he felt truly understood him, and he wanted to understand them. Now he felt the little voices in his head prodding him to take a good look around while he had the chance. Unfortunately, apart from the little snowglobe paperweight, the whole desk looked like files. He picked up the top file. It was thick and heavy. Inside there were dozens of 21Bs. He put it down, then picked up the next file. It was filled with thousands of copies of a form printed in considerably less dense language entitled "Form 21A - Pre-Decedent Acknowledgement and Waiver of Liability." Nathan didn't bother to read it but instead opened the next file, which read "Form 21C - Waiver of Waiver of Liability." The next file was "Form 21D - Waiver of Waiver of Waiver of Liability."

He was just getting to Form 21E ("Request For Delivery Of Waiver of Waiver of Waiver of Liability Form," which required the signatures of an extraordinary seven different functionaries) when the door rematerialized and Nathan hastily put the Form 21E folder back. The frumpy woman re-emerged from the door followed by a newcomer - a large, tall, blond woman in a suit with painted nails and an extremely fixed smile on her face.

"Hello," the new woman said brightly when she saw Nathan. "I'm Donna. First, let me reassure you that I have full managerial authority." Her voice was at least two octaves too high.

"Um... okay," Nathan said. "I'm Nathan Haynes."

"Why are we standing?" Donna continued cheerily. "So formal. Have a seat."

As she said this, two chairs materialized into existence behind them, with a coffee table appearing between them. Nathan gratefully sat down. Donna did the same.

"Can I offer you anything? Coffee? Tea?"

"Oh, I'm fine." Nathan said quickly.

"Come now, you've been through such an ordeal. You need something to calm your nerves. Why not have a drink?"

"Alright. Coffee then," Nathan answered.

"Wonderful," Donna replied brightly. A coffee tray materialized into being on the table along with a few cups and a pitcher. Donna leaned over and started to pour out two cups. As she did this, Nathan noticed that the frumpy woman had retaken her seat behind her desk and was staring at Donna with the same look of disdain that she'd fixed him with. Nathan got the strange impression that really the last thing she wanted to do in life (or unlife) was fetch her supervisor, and she very much hated Nathan for having made her do so.

Donna passed him a small whitish ceramic cup filled with coffee. Nathan took a sip. It tasted slightly stale but strong.

"Would you like something to go with your coffee?" she asked merrily. "Here, have a stick of gum."

Nathan was not accustomed to gum with coffee, and indeed found the idea slightly repulsive, but decided it would be rude to refuse. He accepted a stick of gum in a little wax paper wrapper from her.

"Now, why don't you tell me what happened to you?" she asked imploringly, her painted nails tapping on the rim of her own coffee cup. "How did you come to die?"

"Well, I was murdered," Nathan explained meekly. "A serial killer came to my house and shot me in the head."

"Really?" Donna's features seemed to be overflowing with faux-sympathy. "You poor dear," she cooed.

"Yes. He knocked on the door and came in and asked me a few questions - told me about how he had to keep up with the other serial killers, you know - and then he shot me."

"How simply awful," Donna interjected sweetly. "And I'll bet you've been having a very tough week."

"I guess so," Nathan said, casting his mind back. "My neighbors have been very loud. One of my neighbors - he's an elderly gentlemen - sometimes he keeps me up all night with the noise he makes."

"Terrible. And were you having a tough time at work?"

"Er, I actually don't have a job. I draw disability benefits. You see, I have brain damage from an accident I had when I was small. It's a brain lesion."

Donna shook her head with tremendous sorrow. "Dreadful."

"Yes. I talked about it with my serial killer and he actually said that he'd been looking for someone with exactly that sort of problem. It removes my instinct for self-preservation, you see, so I gather he thought I was just the kind of person he ought to be killing."

"And he discriminated against you!" gasped Donna, horror written across her face. "Wicked, terrible. And did you leave any family behind?"

"No. My family died when I was little, for the most part."

"And you're an orphan! You poor dear," she repeated.

Nathan frowned. He was not exactly an orphan, but before he had chance to explain the complicated circumstances surrounding his family history, Donna started to speak.

"Well, I'm sure that this has all been very, very awful, but you're quite safe now," she said, her tone switching from sympathetic to bright and merry. "If you could just do me one teensy little favor - I'm afraid we need you to sign this form. It's paperwork, I know, but it's terribly necessary. It'll only take a moment. Could you just put your signature right down there for me?"

She slid a 21B - Decedent Acknowledgement and Waiver of Liability across the little coffee table towards Nathan. Nathan frowned at Donna. He was beginning to think that she had been buttering him up.

"Ah, about that," Nathan said. "I said I didn't want to sign the form."

Donna's expression went from warm and friendly to cold in about half a second.

"Why not?" she demanded.

"I just don't want to," Nathan said. "I saw a report on the news that said you shouldn't sign things haphazardly."

"Sign it," she said harshly. Her eyes flashed and her painted nails strained against the handle of her little ceramic coffee cup.

"No," Nathan replied stubbornly.

Donna fixed him with a look of absolute loathing, then slowly rose from her chair.

"Well, we'll see about that," she said. She turned on her heel and walked out of the room through the doorway that briefly appeared to allow her to do so. When she left, the coffee table, the coffee, the tray, the cups, and both of the comfy chairs vanished, sending Nathan plummeting to the floor. The stick of gum, however, remained. Nathan caught this and pocketed it, feeling that it was a shame to let it go to waste.

He was once again alone in the room with the frumpy woman.

"Where did Donna go?" he asked her.

The woman ignored him and continued to stare at the file she had been reviewing. Nathan felt this was quite rude. He might have been dead, but that didn't mean she could treat him like he didn't exist.

He stood up and dusted himself off and waited for something to happen.

Chapter 3

The next few minutes passed in silence. The frumpy woman occasionally looked up from her desk and assumed a series of facial expressions that told Nathan she wished he was a bug so she could squash him. Nathan tried to assume some sort of counter-expression that conveyed that he thought she was being on the whole unnecessarily unpleasant about this whole thing, and that he hadn't asked for any of this, but this proved to be too complicated to get across. Instead, Nathan ended up with his face contorted into something that made him look like one of the bugs that the frumpy woman hoped he would turn into, which Nathan felt was a step in the wrong direction, so he quickly dropped it.

Eventually this tense nonverbal exchange was broken when a door appeared, and a dark-haired man in a crisp black suit and tie walked through it. As the door disappeared, Nathan realized the man's tie was done up into the immensely complicated triple windsor knot, a method of tie-tying known only to the managers of managers. He was tall and had the certain joint aura of authority and hopelessness that mid-tier officials walked around with. Clearly, this man was Donna's manager.

"My name is Ian," he said briskly.

Ian held out his hand. Nathan moved to grab it, but before he could, Ian said:

"I should explain that the handshake is a greeting ritual involving the mutual grasping of hands."

"Er, yes," Nathan agreed, and shook Ian's hand.

"I am Donna's manager," Ian added, confirming Nathan's suspicions. "She said that you wouldn't sign your 21B."

"That's right," Nathan said.

"Allow me to explain that a manager is someone who supervises others," Ian continued.

"Yes, I think I knew that."

Ian's face brightened. "Did you? Well well, I'm sure we can get this all sorted out in good order, then. Let's just take a look at this 21B together, shall we?"

Nathan looked down, half-expecting the chairs to reappear, but they remained stubbornly nonexistent. Ian plucked a 21B from the desk (the frumpy woman gave him a masterfully hate-filled look as he did this, but Ian ignored it). He slapped it expertly with the back of his hand.

"Now, this is the 21B - Decedent Acknowledgement and Waiver of Liability," he said matter-of-factly.

"Yes it is," Nathan confirmed.

"And you don't want to sign it."

"No I don't."

"Ah. I think I see the problem here." He smiled with self-satisfaction. "It's a simple misunderstanding. By signing this form, you acknowledge that you understand that you are dead, and waive all liability that we might incur from any injuries you might sustain, etc., while you are here. I expect Donna already told you this."

Nathan was fairly sure that Donna hadn't told him anything whatsoever, but he nodded in confirmation just to keep things going. He had a funny feeling that this could take a while.

"Good," Ian continued, in an increasingly smug way. "But you still won't sign it?"

"No."

Nathan wondered how many times he would have to repeat this point; Ian's mental faculties seemed to approximate those of a particularly talkative chipmunk.

"Well I think I see the problem here. You can't sign the form because, of course, you have to acknowledge that you are dead to sign it and clearly, you don't understand what death is. Allow me to explain that death is the termination of a life, in your case, your life. You previously died and now have come here, so you see it's alright to sign the form."

"I understood what death is," Nathan said politely.

"Did you? Good, good. Then perhaps you don't understand what liability is. Liability is-"

"I also understand what liability is."

Ian looked thunderstruck.

"Then why can't you pick up the pen and sign-" Then suddenly, he broke into a smile. He grinned broadly and clapped himself on the forehead. "Of course!" he said. His smile grew very condescending. "Let me explain what a pen is. A pen is a writing implement loaded with ink, which, when applied to something like paper-"

"I know what a pen is," intervened Nathan. "And paper, and words, and contracts, and signatures, and everything else for that matter."

"You do?" asked Ian incredulously. "Then why can't you sign the form?"

Nathan paused.

"I guess I don't really see why it's entirely necessary."

"AH! You don't understand why it's necessary. Yes, so that's what you don't understand. Oh yes, it all makes good sense now. Well, we'll fix you right up. I'll give you the tour. Then you'll understand why it's necessary."

Nathan was not entirely sure he agreed with this line of reasoning but he felt tired of arguing, and he was starting to sense that maybe talking to this man wasn't entirely advisable. He rooted around in his pocket to try to find something to occupy his mouth so he would remember not to talk. His fingers closed on the stick of gum Donna had given him. He popped it into his mouth. It was very minty.

Meanwhile, Ian had turned towards the door, which had obligingly reasserted itself as a physical object. Ian courteously held it open.

"After you," he said.

Nathan stepped through it. The desk, the frumpy woman, and the vast forms all vanished. He found himself in a long, well-lit corridor much like one might find in an office, except it had no doors and instead of walls there was an infinite soul-consuming darkness. Ian appeared behind Nathan shortly thereafter. Ian started to stride purposefully down the hall and Nathan followed, although as far as he could see there was nowhere to go.

"We are the bureaucrats," Ian explained as they walked. "It is our job to keep everything running smoothly and in accordance with the law."

"The law?" Nathan asked.

"Let me explain that laws are rules that must be followed," Ian said.

"I know that-"

"Then why did you ask?" Ian asked with a frown.

"But what laws? And why do they need bureaucrats?"

Ian laughed.

"Why do we need bureaucrats? Let me show you something, Mr. Haynes."

A doorway appeared on Ian's left and they went through it. Inside was a room with a quizillion forms in it.

It should be explained for readers who might not be familiar with the concept that a quizillion is defined as the highest number anyone can possibly think of that is not infinity. It is distinguished from *infinity plus one* because unlike *infinity plus one* it cannot be used to win arguments with children.

Naturally, a quizillion forms is, therefore, very many forms indeed. Indeed it is such a mind-bogglingly huge number that the sight of them would have driven a normal man's brain spinning like a hamster in a wheel, if the hamster had just noticed a Sumatran tiger was on the wheel with it. In other words, a normal person would have gone quite insane. Fortunately for Nathan, because he already had brain damage, he merely suffered hysterical loss of taste.

Nathan paused while chewing. His gum had suddenly stopped being minty.

Ian, oblivious to the psychosomatic turmoil he had inflicted on Nathan's poor mind and taste buds, gestured to the quizillion forms with pride.

"You don't think reality simply happens, do you, Mr. Haynes? Dear me no - there's an awful lot of paperwork involved. Why the 2Cs alone - that's authorization for masses to gravitate towards one another - have an entire division devoted to them. And don't even get me started on the 44Fs - that's a request to form a time-like curve... Every single one of these forms had to be prepared by a bureaucrat, Mr. Haynes. That's what we do."

He beamed at the forms, then clapped Nathan on the shoulder.

"Let me show you some of the staff in action."

Much to the relief of Nathan's temporal lobe, the room

disappeared and they were standing back in the hallway. Ian directed Nathan through another door and a room much like the frumpy woman's appeared, except instead of the frumpy woman, a haggard-looking glasses-wearing man was sitting behind the desk, and instead of a snowglobe he had a large plush kitten on top of one of his stacks of forms. The haggard man paid them no attention whatsoever.

"This is where we process 20As," Ian said proudly, pointing to a very small pile of forms on the desk. "Those are Form 20As - Request for True Love. I should explain that love-"

"I know what love is. What are those?" Nathan asked, pointing to a much taller adjacent pile.

"Those are Form 20Bs - Request for Fake Love."

"And, um, what are those?" Nathan pointed to the third and by far the tallest stack on the desk.

"Those are Form 20Cs - Request to Form a Relationship Based On Desperation."

Nathan frowned and picked up a Form 20C. It was written in significantly larger type than the 21B he had been offered in the frumpy woman's room. The first question read, "would you describe your relationship as based on 1) clingy desperation or 2) desperate clinginess (check all that apply.)" His eyes flitted down to the bottom of the page. "Is your sense of desperation based on fear of death? If not, explain."

"You can keep that if you'd like to fill it out later," Ian said magnanimously.

"No thanks," Nathan said, and put it back down on the pile.

The room dissolved around them and they were back in the hallway. Ian led him through another door. This was filled with dozens of desks, each with one or two mildly grim-faced bureaucrats who were pouring over forms with what appeared to be microscopes.

"This is our research and development bureau," Ian said, gesturing broadly. "Here, our hard-working researchers have discovered a new and smaller font size, hitherto unknown to bureaucracy. We have already introduced it on a trial basis on some of our forms. We expect it to reduce paper usage by up to fifty percent."

"Very good," Nathan said. He felt that he ought to say something more at this point, so he asked, "does everything have to have a form?"

"Oh yes," Ian said. "Absolutely everything. Nothing at all happens unless the paperwork has been taken care of. That's what I'm trying to impress upon you, Mr. Haynes. Not a butterfly flaps its wings or a car horn beeps or a second of time ticks by until the appropriate forms are filled in."

"And, that's all done here, is it?"

"No, this is just the central office," Ian said cheerily. "We have branch offices in heaven, hell, purgatory, and New York."

"Er, why do you have an office in New York?"

"Well, we simply wouldn't be a respectable operation if we didn't have an office in New York, even if the rent is extortionate. It's our nicest office. Just between you and me, I wish they would shut down the hell office. All our paper forms kept catching fire there. It's a nightmare. We had to start making documents out of asbestos."

Nathan was not entirely sure whether Ian was being serious or not.

Ian next led him to another little room. Inside it there were about a hundred desks, each of which had a long line of dozens of people waiting in front of it.

"And here is where we process new arrivals," Ian explained. "That is to say, the recently deceased."

"This doesn't look like the room I came from," Nathan said.

"No, of course not. There's no need for them to fill out a 21B. All these people have already signed."

"They have?"

"Yes. Nearly everyone does at one point or another in their lives. It's very rare to get someone like you, who hasn't."

Ian did not elaborate.

"Why are the lines so long?"

"Long?" Ian laughed. "My dear Mr. Haynes, these lines aren't long at all. This is the abbreviated system for processing new arrivals. People in these lines just have to sign a simple 19F, and then initial 25Es, Fs, and Gs, then 30s in triplicate, then a few simple waivers from the hundred series, then a 204 or two, then file sixteen Form 16s-"

"-but why-"

"-then initial the forms attached to their files - just to acknowledge that they are accurate - then P14 if they were born before 1982, or P15 if they were born after - unless they're a child, of course, in which case they need to wait for a parent or guardian to die to assist them-"

"-uh-"

"It's the absolute peak of efficiency!" Ian declared emphatically.

"But why aren't there any people over there?"

Nathan pointed down at the far end of the room, where there were a few desks that were totally without lines. Each had a rather bored looking clerk sitting behind it.

"Oh, I'm glad you asked. Those are our Unlikely Death

Forms desks. They are exclusively for people who die in very specific ways - ways that we expect to kill lots of people but don't happen very often. That one, for example, is the Smallpox Desk."

He pointed to the closest one, which had an aged-looking woman in glasses seated behind it.

"I should explain that smallpox is an infectious disease-"

"Er, wasn't smallpox eradicated?"

"Was it? Goodness, that would explain the lack of business. And next is the Nuclear Disasters desk."

A chirpy young man waved to them from behind the desk and grinned. His teeth glowed green.

Ian waved back and then continued on.

"And this is the Ebola desk," he said. "Fred's the Ebola chief. Say hello, Fred."

"Pleased to meet you," said a bureaucrat from behind the desk. He coughed into his hands. A little blood tinged his palms. Then he reached out, offering a handshake.

"Nice to meet you too," Nathan said, avoiding the handshake.

"This," Ian said, indicating the second-to-last desk in the line, "is the Desk for People Who Died of Badger Attack While Simultaneously Having A Stroke And A Bathtub Fall On Their Heads."

Nathan blinked.

"Is that likely?"

"Oh, we're expecting quite a run on it."

He looked at the woman behind the Badger-Attack-Stroke-And-Falling-Bathtub-Death station. She was a severe-looking middle-aged woman in a mauve blouse with a terribly imperious expression on her face. Nathan got the feeling that it was very foolish indeed to suggest that this was not a good way to die in front of her.

"Busy week, Jeanne?" Ian asked the woman conversationally.

"I had one arrival," she said tersely. "He died of an intracerebral hemorrhage while an old imperial clawfoot fell on him and a honey badger mauled his neck."

"Did you process him?"

"Of course not. The honey badger isn't a true badger. I sent him back to general receiving." She tutted.

"Good, good."

Ian nodded approvingly and turned to go.

"What's that one for?" Nathan asked, pointing to the last desk in the row. The desk was the same, but the station was otherwise very different from the others. There were no papers on it, only a surface of blank, dusty wood, and no clerk sat behind it - all there was to greet an arrival was an empty chair.

Nathan immediately got the impression that he said something he shouldn't have. As soon as Nathan asked about it, all of the clerks from the nearby desks turned and gave him, then each other, dark looks - as if he had just been invited over to an unfamiliar family's house for Thanksgiving and inquired after a little old aunt in a picture who turned out to have run away to become a Somali pirate.

Ian glanced at the empty desk only momentarily before turning away.

"That is the desk for dealing with affairs pertaining to Mr. Travis Erwin Habsworth, of 2388 Shillington Road, Albany," Ian answered quietly.

"Who-"

"Let's go!" the bureaucrat suddenly said very loudly. "Lots

to do. Other places to see. Like this filing cabinet!" He said, ushering Nathan over to a filing cabinet on the other end of the room. "A filing cabinet is a place where we keep files! See?" He yanked it open. It was empty.

Nathan stared at it.

"Er... where we usually keep files," Ian stuttered. He slid the filing cabinet shut. The label on the door read, "Form 404A - Request For More Forms."

"Oh dear," continued Ian. "We'll have to get that fixed. But I think you get the gist of it. Why don't we move on?"

No sooner had he spoken than the room dissolved around them and they were standing back in the hallway.

"And this is the corridor," Ian continued. "Allow me to explain that a corridor is an avenue that connects other rooms."

"I knew that too," Nathan confirmed sardonically.

"Good! Well, I think you've now seen everything of importance. Do you understand why you have to sign your 21B now?"

"No. I don't understand at all."

Ian's genial grin fell.

"You don't?"

"No," Nathan repeated. "I mean, it was all very interesting," he said, trying to spare Ian's feelings. "And thank you for showing it all to me. But I see that you have a lot of forms that are being filled out and that lots of people are working to make sure they are filled out properly, but I'm not sure I understand why you need them filled out, exactly."

For a moment, Ian stood there dumbstruck. He looked confounded, like a dog that has just seen the cat it was chasing escape by helicopter. Then, he shrugged his shoulders.

"I see, I see. There is someone who can explain, but - Oh,

well, there's nothing else for it. We'll just have to go visit him."

"Who?"

"We will have to go see *my* supervisor, Mr. Haynes." He started off down the corridor and then paused. "I should explain that I don't at all like going to see my supervisor."

Nathan followed him, with more than a little trepidation.

Chapter 4

At the very end of the endless corridor, a door appeared, and Ian - now with a distinctly unhappy look - opened it. Nathan walked through and found himself in an expansive office.

It had a line of about a half-dozen chairs on Nathan's right and left. Together with a pair of potted plants, they formed a path of blue carpet that led up to a stately hardwood desk which would have been large enough to accommodate several men - but only one man sat behind it.

The proceedings of the immensely complex field of corporate sociology have yet to explain exactly why it is that businessmen wear ties. The tie is a piece of clothing that serves no known useful purpose. It does not keep the neck warm, nor does it keep the shirt from falling off, nor does it secure the collar to the shirt, nor even does it act as a counterweight to the heavy items that you might reasonably have in your back pocket. The tie therefore does nothing. Most women have quite sensibly forgone ties in favor of their own totally impractical and inexplicable garments, like high heels.

After tinkering with the hypothesis that it must be used to keep some sort of devious shirt-python from jumping down your collar and biting you on the chest, corporate sociologists disregarded this - and indeed all snake-related tie theorems - and concluded that the tie must be a status symbol. While they have yet to entirely decipher the meanings of many individual ties, the sociologists concluded that the tie must be used to signal rank and authority to unfamiliar members of the corporate structure. Therefore, it must be possible to ascertain exactly how powerful a person is from his tie. A simple errand monkey, for example, might only wear a tie with a half-windsor knot, while a middle manager has a tie with the immensely complicated triple windsor knot.

The man behind the hardwood desk was not wearing a tie. A little shiver went up Nathan's spine. Such men are dangerous.

The tieless man was very large, perhaps six and a half feet tall, wearing a gray suit and a bare white collar. His hair was silver-gray and there was a predatory glint in his dark, merciless eyes. He did not look genial or friendly or accommodating like Ian. In fact, he looked like the opposite of all those things. His finger tips were pressed together contemplatively.

"Mr. Nathan Haynes," he called out. "Welcome."

"Am I?" Nathan asked, with surprise.

"No, not at all. In fact, Mr. Haynes, you are very, very unwelcome. I understand you have caused some problems in receiving, but I do not want to hear about them. I would prefer it if you shriveled up into a little ball of nothing and disappeared into even more nothing. But there are pleasantries that have to be observed, so I am going to pretend otherwise."

"I have been expecting you," he added, after a suitable interval. "Donna told me what happened." He pointed to the nearest seat, where Donna was quietly seated, her lips pursed.

"I have been observing your progress," the tieless man continued.

Nathan could not immediately see how he might have done this, but he knew better than to ask.

"I'll just be going then, shall I?" Ian said with a fixed grin. He started towards the door.

"No, sit," the tieless man said. "Both of you."

Nathan sat down as quickly as he could. Ian did the same, looking very nervous.

"I am Director Fulcher," the collarless man said. "You are Nathan Haynes. Is that right?"

Nathan nodded.

"Now, I understand that you have refused to sign your 21B."

"Yes," Nathan agreed. "I guess I just don't see the point of all these forms and signing and whatnot."

"Ah, but Ian has already explained it to you, hasn't he? The universe has laws, doesn't it, Mr. Haynes? These laws don't just enforce themselves. It's us - the bureaucrats - that make it all happen. We are here to make sure that proper procedure is followed, and until every form is filled out, and every 'i' dotted and 't' crossed, things simply cannot be allowed to proceed."

"You mean that you have to fill out forms for everything in the whole universe?"

"Yes."

Nathan was not quite sure he understood what Director Fulcher meant.

"So - er - butterflies in springtime?"

"Each one needs a form."

"And beautiful sunsets?"

"There is a form for that as well."

"And a sense of profound happiness and fulfillment?"

"One hundred and sixteen different forms and a public consultation, at the absolute minimum," Fulcher confirmed solemnly. "The whole vastness of creation, from blazing suns to tiny atoms of hydrogen, every object from the minuscule to the awesome - every event, from two little molecules of gas bumping into each other to galaxy-shattering supernovas - must have its paperwork properly filled out."

"Er... and what happens if you don't fill out the proper forms?"

"They do not happen."

Nathan sat there in his chair, dumbstruck. The ramifications of this were mindbending, and as it turned out, his mind was quite rigid from the traumas (lesions, quizillions of forms, and gunshot wounds) that it had already suffered through and was not prepared to process it. Do not think about how or why bureaucrats would run reality, it told him. Think about this cereal jingle instead. It played him several seconds of catchy music from an old television cereal commercial while he pleasantly hallucinated about cartoon breakfast mascots, while the rationalization department of his mind hurriedly tried to come up with an acceptable interpretation of what Fulcher was telling him. By the end of the jingle, here is what it had come up with:

"What does any of that have to do with me?" Nathan asked. This, the rationalization department had decided, would allow him to handily ignore the problem.

Unfortunately, Director Fulcher did not answer "nothing at all - you may go now," which is the answer the rationalization part of the brain always secretly hopes for but never receives when it directs your mouth to ask this question.

Instead, Fulcher did what usually happens when this question is asked and sighed heavily, then leaned back in his chair with a nostalgic look in his eye.

"Ah yes," he said airily. "What does it have to do with you? Well to answer that, we have to go all the way back. Way back to the very beginning. We bureaucrats have always been around. In the beginning, the paperwork was very manageable."

"Are you talking about the beginning of the universe?"

"You may call it what you like. Then there was rather a tremendous explosion in our workload. I understand you have heard of it on your side of things."

"Do you mean, the Big Bang?"

Fulcher did not answer but continued to muse.

"Things got pretty complicated after that. We had to invent all kinds of new forms to keep up with the law - which back then was rapidly changing. Our workload got bigger and bigger as creation got larger and larger."

"You mean to tell me that you've been filing forms for - for everything? Since the beginning of the universe?" Nathan gaped. His mind slipped back to the quizillion forms he had seen in the storage room, but then quickly caught itself and started playing the cereal jingle again, his memory defaulting to the wholly more sane image of a cartoon leprechaun trying to sell him marshmallows.

"It was quite a lot of work. Fortunately, we discovered a loophole in the law. It turns out that as long as an object is very small, we don't actually have to file paperwork for it unless someone requests the relevant forms - so most things have no paperwork at all, and if anyone asks for it we just file it on the spot. Useful, eh?"

"I guess?"

"But even given that," Fulcher powered forward, "our workload eventually grew too great. The universe, you see, kept growing, and in the end there just weren't enough hours in the day to file all the necessary forms to keep reality running at the high operational standards that we have maintained from the beginning. We started to make compromises.

Simplifications for the sake of efficiency. We slowed down time to make things easier on ourselves."

"You slowed down-"

"But in the end, we realized this couldn't continue. And that is where you come in, Mr. Haynes. You and everyone else."

"It - it is?"

"Yes. But I am afraid I cannot tell you any more until you fill out your 21B."

"I don't want to." Nathan said stubbornly.

Fulcher stood abruptly, eyes blazing. Ian and Donna cowered back and away from him.

"Surely you must see how important this is, Mr. Haynes."

"No, I don't. I don't understand at all. Does everyone have to sign these forms?"

"Most people already signed theirs before they arrived, Mr. Haynes."

"They did?"

"Oh yes. To be honest I am surprised that you haven't. But anyone who has ever signed a car lease or rental agreement - or signed an overlong employment agreement - or clicked the - 'agree' button on an end-user license agreement without reading it has pre-signed their Waiver."

"Well, that explains it. I don't really like signing things. I saw this report on the news about someone using these agreements to steal houses-"

"The exact reasons are unimportant," Fulcher said with a dismissive wave of his hand. "But everyone has to sign a Waiver. I must insist that you sign your 21B."

Nathan shook his head rapidly. He wasn't even sure why he was refusing, except on the pure principle of stubbornness, and because his intuition told him that it was a bad idea. To be fair, this intuition came from the same consciousness that kept playing him cereal jingles, so maybe its judgment was not to be entirely trusted... but Nathan decided to stick to his refusals all the same.

"I see." Director Fulcher said, drawing himself up to his full height. "I see," he repeated. "Well, there's only one thing to do then."

"You're going to send me to see your supervisor?" Nathan asked, remembering that "I see, I see," was exactly what Ian had said before doing just that.

Fulcher gave him a grim smile. "I'm afraid that you are not allowed to see my supervisor unless you have been canonized. Although she has very recently started meeting nobel peace prize winners. Have you won a Nobel Peace Prize, Mr. Haynes?"

"Not as far as I remember," Nathan said uncertainly. "In fact, now that you mention it, I don't think I've won a Nobel Prize of any kind." He felt a bit embarrassed.

"Not even economics?" Fulcher inquired.

"Not even economics," Nathan confirmed.

"Well, then I am afraid you cannot see *my* supervisor, Mr. Haynes."

"Should we keep him here, sir?" Donna asked, speaking up for the first time. She was glaring at Nathan with a mixture of anger and malice. "Can't we just plop him back in station four until he agrees to sign his 21B?"

"No, of course not," Fulcher said, straightening his collar. "If he hasn't signed his liability waiver, we can't have him here. He might sue us. No, we will have to send him back."

"Back?" Nathan asked.

"Yes, back," Fulcher said. "To life."

"Oh, that sounds like a very good idea," Nathan said, nodding. "I have to finish doing my laundry."

Fulcher fixed him with a rather wolfish smile. Nathan had a nasty feeling he was about to find out why Director Fulcher didn't wear a tie.

"Dear me, Mr. Haynes, you didn't think that we would send you back to life as yourself, did you? No, no, no. I was thinking of sending you back as a worm."

"A worm!" exclaimed Nathan. "But I don't think I would enjoy being a worm."

"No, I don't think you would either," Fulcher said, smiling. "That is the point. But I think we could find something you would enjoy even less. Maybe, for example, we could send you back as an eel."

"An eel?" Nathan gasped with horror. In truth, his mind had not yet processed what it would be like to be an eel, and his mouth - while resentfully expressing the opinion that it was always picking up the slack and doing all the work around here - was simply repeating everything that Fulcher said. Fulcher, perhaps sensing this, began to elaborate.

"Yes, an eel. A filthy, slimy, self-conscious eel that no one wants to touch. An electric eel, I should think, so one day, when you are particularly yearning for human contact, a curious little girl will pick you up out of the water as she swims, but you will shock her without meaning to, and she will run away crying."

"Oh no!"

"Yes!" Fulcher said, his eyes flashing triumphantly. "And then you will be speared by an Indonesian eel fisherman, who will sell your meat at a fish market to a young woman who will cook you, decide you taste bad, and throw you away."

"That sounds very unpleasant," Nathan said.

"Or maybe," Fulcher continued, with a manic glint in his eye, "we should bring you back as a tapeworm."

"Not a tapeworm!"

"Yes, a tapeworm! A tapeworm that prefers to eat meat, but it lives in the gut of a cow, and the cow only eats grass, and you shall have to spend the whole of your life wishing just once you could have a bite of bacon rather than filthy, tasteless, grass."

"That does sound unpleasant," Nathan said.

"Or maybe we shall bring you back-" Fulcher paused dramatically, and Nathan knew that he had saved the very worst for last "-as a fat man!"

"Not a fat man!"

"Yes, a fat man! A fat man who has a genuine gland problem - the only fat man alive who actually has a gland problem! A gland problem that is totally incurable by modern medical science. And no matter what you do, you will gain more and more weight, and never be able to convince anyone that it is actually not your fault!"

"Nooooooo!" protested Nathan.

"Yes!" countered Fulcher dramatically.

"Nooooooooooo," shot back Nathan.

"Yesss!" replied Fulcher.

"Nooooooooooooooo," argued Nathan.

"Yessss," insisted Fulcher. "But of course, all of this could be avoided, and you should never have to be an eel or a tapeworm or a fat man, if only you will sign your Form 21B. Then you would be able to stay here, and never be any of those things."

But Nathan was having none of that.

"I won't sign the form," he said. "Even if I have to be an eel and a tape worm and a fat man."

Fulcher considered him briefly, and in a flash of realization, Nathan knew the Director had one last trump card to play.

"What if the fat man was also big boned? Genuinely big-boned! The only fat man alive who really has big bones!"

Nathan reeled in horror at the merciless sadism of his opponent, but he still refused to yield. If only out of sheer stubbornness, he would not sign the form. After all, he had said he wouldn't sign it before, so he couldn't very well switch positions at this point.

"I won't sign the form even if you bring me back as a big-boned fat man with glandular problems. Not even if you bring me back with twelve aunts."

Fulcher regarded him shrewdly.

"Your resolve is stronger than I thought. I respect that. We will send you back to life!" He reached into his desk and pulled out a form.

"You are sending him back as the eel?" Donna asked breathlessly.

"Or the tapeworm?" Ian asked.

"Or the fat man?" Nathan inquired.

"No," Fulcher said. "I was bluffing. There's a terrible lot of paperwork involved in bringing someone back to life as something he's not supposed to be, so I will have to bring you back as yourself. To bring you back as an eel or a tapeworm or a fat man I would need -" his expression darkened "-to ask for a favor from another department. And you aren't worth that. So I'm sending you back as-is."

Nathan practically choked with relief.

"But Director," Ian began nervously. "He was shot in the head. If you send him back as is he'll just immediately die again and come back here."

Fulcher waved the problem aside.

"I will give him one of the replica bodies we use when we have to enter the living world or visit the New York office," he said. "He won't die immediately." He began to fill out the immensely complex resurrection form with astonishing speed. After a few seconds he said, "As soon as I sign this form you will be sent back to the world of the living. But mark my words, Mr. Haynes, I run a very smooth operation. Every form in my department is filed. Every 'e' is dotted and 't' crossed!"

"You mean every 'i' is dotted?" Nathan inquired.

"That too! And I will have your form appropriately signed and filed, sir, even if it takes me all of my directorial cunning. You have not heard the last of me, Mr. Haynes."

Nathan was not listening. His brain had started playing the cereal jingle again.

Fulcher signed the form. Nathan disappeared.

The last thing he heard before reappearing in the world of the living (after the ending of the jingle) was Fulcher's voice.

"Ian, find Brian and bring him to my office immediately. I have a job for him."

And then Nathan crossed over the pale barrier of souls that separates worlds and found himself unexpectedly, and against the odds, alive.

Chapter 5

Nathan Haynes was a lifelong resident of the very sorry city of Dead Donkey, Nevada. It was one of the very worst places to live in the whole of the United States, and indeed much of Nevada.

The city had been founded in the mid-1860s by a certain Efrain Smith, a settler from back East who decided to go West to seek his fortune in the great California gold rush. Smith was a particularly extraordinary man for two reasons: first, because he preferred the company of his donkey, Arnie, to humans, and second, because he failed to hear that the California gold rush had ended some ten years before he set out (and that the American Civil War was pretty much over). He also got spectacularly lost while trying to make his way to California and ended up trudging around in a series of vast, nightmarish circles, despite the fact that Arnie the donkey kept reorienting towards San Francisco and straining to lead him in that direction, and that passing settlers kept telling him he was going the wrong way. He refused to believe either the settlers or his donkey (what, he asked, did a donkey know?) and ended up spending more than two years walking but getting nowhere. Smith also had a compass, but he refused to believe it because it co-opted the donkey's story, which led him to believe that they must be conspiring against him somehow.

Eventually, poor Arnie's health gave out and the donkey had keeled over right in the middle of a vast, desolate plain. Since Arnie had been carrying all of his stuff, Efrain Smith had decided to end his journey right on the spot and thereby founded the city of Dead Donkey.

Dead Donkey, as previously mentioned, is not a very nice

place to live. Its skyline consists of some of the ugliest, bleakest, most twisted buildings in the world, many of which are either painted dull gray or the exact shade (and smell) of vomit. It has one of the highest rates of crime in the world. Efrain Smith technically founded it in California, but California refused to take it, invoking the secret clause in the US constitution that allows any state to transfer any territory to Nevada for any reason. (This is the same reason that Reno is in Nevada.)

Dead Donkey has a population of some tens of thousands and would be one of the larger cities in Nevada, except it is not really a city. It is technically classified as a garbage dump. Dead Donkey's mayor (or to give him his legally proper title, Garbage Dump Supervisor), insists this is because of a meaningless technicality in the law, and is in no way because the statutory salary of a garbage dump supervisor is greater than that of a mayor.

The mayor of Dead Donkey is not very popular.

Along with many other crimes, like murder, fraud, and Muleball (which we will get to shortly), arson is rampant in Dead Donkey. In fact, the arson rate in Dead Donkey is the highest in the world. The city's public policy analysts have come up with various reasons this might be - the high rate of unemployment, alcoholism and smoking, economic stagnation, a culture of gang violence among the youths, the very high average temperature of Dead Donkey exacerbated by global warming, the proliferation of dry brush and whatnot around the city, the generally inadequate amount of rain the city receives, general lack of smoke detectors, poor enforcement, bad building codes, etc.

None of these reasons are correct. The actual cause of Dead

Donkey's arson problem is the extremely high number of arsons committed by public policy analysts, who have long since worked out that as long as there's an arson problem for them to explain, they'll all be able to keep their extremely cushy and high-paying think-tank jobs. While some have protested this to the mayor, he insists that the public policy analysts are all friends of his and they wouldn't possibly be doing anything so insidious, and the arsons must all be down to the confluence of sunspots, just as the latest public policy analysis said.

The mayor of Dead Donkey is not very popular.

Dead Donkey's curious predilection for arson was best summed up by 'Sandy' Drexler, the most famous of Dead Donkey University's poet laureates who had neither gone insane or tried to escape by mailing themselves to Baltimore, which is an increasingly common problem among Dead Donkey's poets. (Fortunately, packages containing members of the latter category are easily spotted because their postal labels are written in rhyming verse.) Drexler's poem went like this:

"My true home is Dead Donkey,
My city bright and fair,
The girls, they set my heart alight,
The boys, they torched my hair."

Over the years, arson had actually become vital to the local economy, with arsons both keeping the local building industry employed, as they tried to rebuild the local skyline almost as fast as it burned down, and bringing firefighters from as far as three counties over to spend money, which represented a vital infusion of capital into Dead Donkey's businesses. While Dead

Donkey was required by law to maintain its own fire department (Nevada's "Statutes Pertaining to High Population Garbage Dumps"), one of the cornerstones of maintaining an arson-based economy was having a terrible local fire department so firefighters from further afield would have to be called in. Dead Donkey's firefighters had no idea how to fight fires. While they often managed to get to the fire itself, that was about the limit of their expertise, and they could often be seen standing outside burning buildings staring at their hoses in puzzlement and despondency. They used their firetruck's sirens exclusively to cut through traffic on their way to the supermarket which was itself rarely, if ever, on fire. Their dog was a dachshund.

In fact, the Dead Donkey Fire Department is so bad that when one of the city's few domestic industries, Dead Donkey's much famed xylophone fence factory was put to light, the factory proprietors did not even bother calling the fire department. Instead, they commissioned the construction of the world's largest air conditioner to attempt to cool the factory faster than the fire could heat it. This worked extremely well until the arsonists set fire to the air conditioner, which at last precipitated the xylophone fence factory's closure, and forced the factory's many customers to look elsewhere for their supply of musical barriers.

Contrary to Efrain Smith's original gold mining and donkey ranching intentions, Dead Donkey neither has a mining nor an agriculture industry. There is no gold in Dead Donkey. Someone once discovered what he thought was a gold mine but the rocks within were later found to be entirely arsenic which in retrospect looked nothing like gold. This may also account for the lack of an agricultural industry, as the only animal that eats the grass around Dead Donkey is a single breed of depressed-looking cow that produces no milk, and whose meat is poisonous.

This was not to say that Dead Donkey's economy was entirely dependent on arson. Tourism was a vital part of the Dead Donkey economy. Travel agencies did a roaring business luring people into the city with promises of free transportation and board, then charging them through the nose to leave as fast as possible.

Dead Donkey is also at the center of Nevada's innovation economy. Many visionaries (a term they vastly prefer to 'crazy kooks') have made their way to the city of Dead Donkey over the years. The aforementioned xylophone fence factory, set up by eccentric billionaire Olivia Doles, who realized she could put an end to all the heavy lugging around of xylophones that people so inconveniently had to do, is but one example. Dead Donkey is also home to the inventors of the world's only car rental agency accessible exclusively by helipad, which stays in business by catering to upscale and extremely stupid clients. Engineers from Dead Donkey university have also recently invented a motorized fork that destroys your food if you are too fat to safely eat it. The manufacturers are eager to point out that this does not technically violate the guarantee on the package that it will "reduce your eating habit." Generally speaking, the economy of Dead Donkey has markedly improved since the 1970s, when the US federal government declared it a disaster area, owing to the dangerously high levels of radiation found in people's air conditioners - later found to extend to the air, and not just the air conditioners. This radiation was later linked to the use of weaponized cesium in the xylophone fence manufacturing process. Thereafter, the city enjoyed something of an economic revival as a center to train psychologists specializing in clinical depression and suicide hotline operators opened downtown, right next to the training center for professional gamblers.

Recent news wasn't all good, though. The US Marine Corps destroyed Dead Donkey's city hall several years ago, after the building's uncanny resemblance to the Ba'athist Party Headquarters in Fallujah led a passing marine colonel to mistakenly believe that Saddam had escaped capture after all and set up shop in Dead Donkey. This misunderstanding was greatly exacerbated by the fact that the city flag of Dead Donkey, by coincidence, is exactly the same as the flag of pre-war Iraq, and the logo that is painted onto government buildings in the city is the exact same emblem as the battle standard of the Fedayeen militia. These coincidences culminated in the marines shelling the city hall with rather a lot of 155mm artillery, which demolished the building and sent the local xylophone fences a-singing with a musical cacophony as the shrapnel pinged off of them.

The mayor's office is now located in Dead Donkey municipal park (one of the world's many parks where a stabbing is the best you can hope for if you decide to visit). More precisely, it is located in the urinals, where a charming sign informs visitors they are standing in "Urinals and Mayor's Office." Due to a number of unfortunate incidents, this sign was amended to read "Please do not urinate on the mayor." After complaints, it was further amended to read, "Please do not urinate on the mayor without due cause."

The mayor of Dead Donkey is not very popular.

Genetic tests have revealed that Arnie the donkey was not in fact a donkey but a mule, which explains the lack of success behind Smith's earlier attempts to breed the poor creature. However, the authorities of Dead Donkey have refused to contemplate a name change, arguing that a city named Dead Mule would just be silly. Arnie's true identity is commemorated in the official and original sport of Dead Donkey, a game called Muleball. The rules of Muleball are not exactly well-defined, but it basically involves two teams of any numbers of players. Members of one team will then endeavor to search for members of the other team and then, when they find one, jump out and beat the everliving crap out of him until he falls unconscious, then haul him to the other side of town (traditionally relieving him of his valuables in the process), whereupon they score one point. The game continues until one team runs out of valuables, and members of one of the teams are usually very surprised to find out they are playing. Nevertheless, it is much beloved by the people. It involves neither mules nor balls.

Arson, while frowned upon in baseball, tennis, wrestling, and so on, is considered perfectly legitimate in Muleball, as well as some particularly corrupt forms of international soccer.

Due to the high attrition to atheism among their clergy, all major churches pulled out of Dead Donkey, usually after a few hours and in one particularly severe case seconds. The last remnant of organized religion in Dead Donkey is the Church of Particularly Cynical Atheists, which maintains a growing if deeply unpleasant presence in the city.

This was not to say everyone hated Dead Donkey. It was extremely popular in a number of select circles, but mostly among the blind community owing to very low property prices and the pleasantly musical nature of its fences. Dead Donkey therefore had a rather large blind community, although the few who had regained their sense of sight through the miracles of modern medicine had run away screaming.

This was Nathan Haynes' home city, the city where he had been born, and the city where he had (recently) died. But, like the city's many poets who tried to mail themselves to Baltimore, he was sent back.

Chapter 6

Nathan resurrected with a faint scrunching noise, like the sound of an autistic woodchuck chucking a log particularly hard into the knee of an unwary passerby. He blinked. He was standing back in his own living room. It was much how he had left it, except he noticed that the floor appeared to be rather bloody, and that his own dead body was inconveniently sprawled across the floor with a neat little hole in the side of its (his?) head. He sighed, scratched his head (which is to say the one that didn't have the bullet in it and was still working) and wondered what to do. He supposed that the first order of business, now that he was back, would have to be getting rid of his body, but he guessed that people weren't simply allowed to dump dead bodies in the trash can and forget about them. There were probably all sorts of pesky rules pertaining to the disposal of biological waste and human remains and whatnot that would get in the way. Nathan supposed he would have to call the police.

He picked up the phone. There was no dial tone.

Then Nathan remembered that the serial killer, before he had killed Nathan, had cut the phone line. Nathan frowned. He remembered objecting to the serial killer's cutting of the phone line at the time, anticipating that it would create some sort of difficulty in the future just like this, but the serial killer had insisted that it was very important.

With a sigh, Nathan went over to his cable drawer.

Virtually every household in the world now has at least one drawer that contains all of the miscellaneous cables that its residents have collected over the years. These include power cables, modem cables, internet cables, cables for cell phones, cables for smartphones, cables for laptops, cables for cameras, cables for lamps and clocks and air conditioners, frayed cables, broken cables, straight cables, curly cables, unknown and inscrutable cables, unspeakable cables, unmentionable cables, eldritch cables coated in paint of an unknown color that siphon off power from the grid to a dead alien god with dark and mysterious purpose, etc.

Even though Nathan did not really trust technology, largely because he did not understand how it worked, he too had a drawer of cables. He waddled over to this drawer (under his desk), and began to root around inside for a new telephone cable. He was sure he had one somewhere, and eventually found it. Then, with much dark muttering about the bother, he replaced the telephone cable.

This, he reflected, was on balance a lot of trouble to go through to restore phone service to his house, particularly since Dead Donkey's phone system barely worked anyway. Owing to the unwillingness of any reputable phone companies to risk their trucks in Dead Donkey's streets, Dead Donkey still used a manual telephone exchange - that is, one of the big networks of boards you see in old-timey movies where a woman in a headset plugs a long metal plug into a little socket to connect your call. This was a problem because the telephone exchange operators did not really know how to operate the telephone exchange, and generally speaking had no idea which socket to plug the little plug into, and would therefore, at best, take a wild guess and connect you to someone else at random. While this was a good way to catch up with the neighbors and the pizzerias (as the case might be), it was very inconvenient for anyone trying to place an urgent call. If this didn't work, the telephone exchange operators would sometimes pretend to be the person you were trying to call rather than connect you and carry on the conversation as best they could, all in the name of maintaining the illusion of telephone service throughout the city.

Nathan knew all this, but he felt there was at least a sixty percent chance that the telephone exchange operators knew which plug was the police, so he felt it was worth a try.

He plugged the new cable in and dialed the police. As far as he could tell, they connected him properly, but then you never could tell. The operators could be tricky. Nathan's half of the conversation went like this.

"Hello," he said. "I would like to report that I have been murdered."

There was a pause.

"Yes," he confirmed. "I was murdered just about a half-hour or so ago, and I wondered if you could come by and pick up my dead body. I'm afraid I don't really know what to do with it."

There was another pause.

"No, I'm not hurt. A serial killer came in and shot me in the head and I died. That's how I was murdered."

There was yet another pause.

"Why yes, I do have a history of serious mental illness. Hello? Hello?"

The emergency operator (or quite possibly the telephone exchange operator), had hung up.

Nathan scratched his head.

He stooped down and grabbed his dead body under the armpits and dragged it out into the backyard, where he had a wheelbarrow that he'd partially filled with dirt for some purpose of gardening that he could no longer remember.

Nathan heaved his corpse onto the wheelbarrow, where its arms remained, hanging loosely over the side. He clapped his hands together to get the dirt off and stepped back into his house.

He was just trying to work out whether the undertaker or a one-way pre-paid freight shipping label to Baltimore was cheaper when there was a knock at Nathan's door. Nathan stood up and blinked, then his brain said something like this.

"Oh, maybe that's the serial killer come back to kill me again. I'd better go get it in case it is."

Then another part of his brain said something like, "But if it is the serial killer then he'll just have to go to all the trouble of killing you again and that's no good because they'll probably send you right back."

Then the first part of his brain said something like,

"Well, if it is the serial killer then you'll just have to explain things to him and tell him he'll just have to go find someone else to kill, because I think that was my last telephone cable, and it will be very inconvenient if he cuts it again and you have to go down to the store to buy another one. Not to mention," it added impetuously, "that there's rather a lot of blood over your nice clean carpet and you still don't know how to get rid of the old dead body from last time."

It waited for the second part of his brain to respond, but no response was forthcoming because the second part of his brain had started playing the cereal jingle again and had gone so far as to co-opt his mouth and lungs into whistling some of the catchier bits. He got pretty well caught up in the whistling until a loud knocking sound disrupted his train of thought.

"Oh dear," went the first part of his brain. "What was that?"

Eventually, after several more whistles and knocks, Nathan exhausted his immediate repertoire of cereal jingles and managed to stagger over to his door. He opened it. There was a single tall policeman standing on his porch.

"Good afternoon, sir," the policeman said politely. "Are you Mr. Nathan Haynes?"

After a quick check with himself, Nathan confirmed that he was.

"You called us and said something about a murder," the policeman said.

"Oh yes," Nathan said brightly. "Maybe you can help me get rid of the body. Come in, come in." He ushered the policeman into his living room and directed him to sit in the least bloodsplattered of the several green chairs he owned. "Can I offer you something? Cerea- er... coffee? Tea?"

"That's very kind of you, but no thank you, sir," the policeman said quietly. "Could you just tell me what happened here?"

Nathan launched into his explanation. He told the policeman about the nice serial killer who had knocked on his door and then shot him in the head, and his subsequent trip to the strange bureaucrats' offices, and the frumpy woman, and Donna, and Ian, and Director Fulcher, and how they had decided to send him back to life. He showed the policeman where the serial killer had shot him, and subsequently where Nathan had dumped his own corpse in his backyard wheelbarrow, and explained about the phone cable and how it would be awfully inconvenient if the serial killer had to cut it again while killing him, since he would have to go out and buy a new one, and he would therefore have to borrow one of his neighbor's cars to go to the store since it was too far to walk and the buses only ran in one direction and the city's only car rental place was only accessible by helipad and all the taxis were a shade too hideously orange to be used by any but the city's large blind population.

The police officer listened to all this in silence and wrote it down in a large notebook. When Nathan had finished his story, the policeman scratched his head.

"It seems to me that you basically need to stop the serial killer from coming back and get rid of the body in your back yard."

"Yes," Nathan agreed vigorously.

"Well, we can take care of all that for you, Mr. Haynes."

"Oh, you can? Good." Nathan was happy that the policeman was taking this in such good stride.

"Yes, we can get your old body taken away to the morgue and post a patrol outside your building so if your killer comes back, we can have him caught in a jiffy and employed."

For readers not familiar with Dead Donkey's criminal justice system, Dead Donkey does not have any municipal prisons. Minor offenders, like jaywalkers, litterers, and guerrilla artists are instead packed off to live in the bad neighborhood of Dead Donkey, where they are condemned to spend the rest of their days complaining loudly to one another about how bad crime has gotten all of a sudden. Major offenders, like murderers, are employed and put to work in the mayor's office.

The mayor of Dead Donkey is not very popular.

Nathan, who didn't pay much attention to civics and hadn't picked up on this particular point (and was in fact listening to the cereal jingle play inside his own head again), simply went, "oh good."

The policemen then recited much of the information that Nathan had told him to check that it was correct, making a few notes here and there when Nathan interrupted him to point out inaccuracies.

"Good," the policeman said when they had finished doing this. "Now I just need you to sign this witness statement."

He handed Nathan the witness statement and a pen.

Nathan clicked the pen. His hand hovered over the signature box.

The print was small. Very small.

The cereal jingle playing in Nathan's head stopped. He frowned.

"Wait a minute. This is a 21B."

The policeman's eyes suddenly became dodgy and evasive.

"If you could just sign the witness statement-"

"You're a bureaucrat, aren't you!" Nathan exclaimed. Suddenly everything fell into place. This explained why the policeman hadn't seemed surprised when Nathan told him his story. It also explained why the "policeman" was wearing a badge that read "Temporary Badge Pending Request For Badge" and why his uniform was yellow rather than blue. Also, he had actually responded to a call, which was rather suspicious for the Dead Donkey police - they usually ran and hid until the crisis was over.

"Blast," the fake policemen murmured, throwing off his cap and jacket. Beneath, he was wearing the unmistakable stiff off-brown suit and tie of a low-level bureaucrat.

Chapter 7

About an hour earlier, back in the office of Director Fulcher, Ian had escorted a very normal looking young man into the room. This young man was wearing the unmistakable stiff off-brown suit and tie of a low-level bureaucrat, and was in fact the same young man who would attempt to deceive Nathan into signing a 21B about an hour later. The young man's name was Brian Dithershoes.

Brian hated his parents. He hated his name. He hated the laughs and jeers of the other boys that he'd had to bear when he was young, and the jibes from the other bureaucrats now that he was a bureaucrat.

He hated being called Brian.

He longed to be called Andrew, in his opinion a vastly superior and much more respectable name as compared to the miserable mockery of a first name that was Brian.

"Brian!" Director Fulcher boomed.

Brian winced at the sound of his own name.

"Yes, Director Fulcher?" he called back, gritting his teeth.

"I have a job for you, and if you do it right, I will grant you what you've always wanted."

"You mean it?" Brian asked, his face lighting up.

"Yes. I'll give you a name change," Fulcher said. "Then you can be called whatever you want. Panny or Fulump or Gwash or Bupper or Adolph. It doesn't matter to me."

Brian's eyes lit up.

"Or Andrew?"

"Yes. Or Andrew."

"Whatever it is, I'll do it."

"Good," Fulcher said. "You will need this." He handed

Brian a small, official satchel, which - going by weight alone - felt like it had several large and particularly obese elephants inside it.

"This contains forms you may need to fill out during your trip to make sure all the paperwork is in order. The form 21B is particularly important."

Brian found the form 21B near the top, right on top of a form EEE - Report of Incident Pertaining to Mr. Travis Erwin Habsworth, of 2388 Shillington Road, Albany.

And then Director Fulcher explained the whole thing to him.

About five minutes later, Brian was on the way to the world of the living, and for him the future had never looked brighter.

No matter what would happen, he would break this Nathan Haynes man. He would force him to sign the 21B, no matter how cruel or treacherous the method, no matter the cost. The form would be signed.

Chapter 8

"Won't you please sign it?" Brian begged.

"No!" Nathan said.

"Please?"

"No!"

"Pretty please?"

"I told you NO! Get out of my house."

"As I have already explained, I can't leave until you have signed your 21B. Please sign it."

"No."

"Why not?"

"Well, for a start, I'm not even dead anymore. Why should I sign a form that acknowledges I am dead when I'm not even dead anymore?"

"It would be doing me a very big favor," Brian said truthfully.

"Too bad! I won't sign it. Now get out!"

"Perhaps you would like to call the police again to get them to throw me out," Brian suggested shiftily.

"Oh no. I'm not falling for that again. Now leave my house before I call the serial killer."

"Do you have the serial killer's phone number?"

Nathan had to admit that he didn't.

"But if you don't leave," he added, "I will go and get my toothbrush!"

The object called a toothbrush in Dead Donkey would nowhere else in the world be identified as a toothbrush. It is in fact, between its crude, unnatural contours and razor-sharp bristles, an instrument to unleash terrible torture on the gums of an unsuspecting victim. The residents of Dead Donkey use them exclusively for self-defense, which accounts for both the extremely high volume of mouthwash sold in the city and the reluctance of even hardened Dead Donkey criminals (or mayor's aides, as they prefer to be called) to conduct home invasions in the early morning or evening, particularly into their victims' bathrooms.

Brian, who was not from Dead Donkey, did not understand this threat and stared blankly at Nathan.

Suddenly, the loud crack of a gunshot made Brian jump.

Nathan sipped his coffee indifferently.

"That's my neighbor, Mr. Fletcher. Very noisy, isn't he?"

"Was that a gunshot?"

"Oh yes, I expect so. I might as well go and see what he's up to, just to make sure that he isn't shooting out streetlights again."

"Why would anyone shoot out streetlights?" Brian asked, mystified.

"He claims that they are much too bright for him to use his night vision goggles," Nathan said matter-of-factly.

Brian was still processing this statement when Nathan put down his cup of coffee and walked out the front door. Brian quickly followed him.

Nathan's neighborhood was very unusual. Maybe it was the collection of run-down cars parked on both sides of the street, at least half of which were on fire, or the graffiti strewn sidewalks, or the empty shell casings that littered the grass, but something somehow suggested to Brian that Nathan did not live in the best neighborhood. The buildings themselves consisted of identical one-story post-fabricated housing units. What made them post-fabricated was that while pre-fabricated units are built ahead of time, broken into pieces, and then assembled, these housing units were all marked to be unassembled, broken into pieces, and then destroyed in a furnace, preferably a particularly hot furnace - hence post-fabricated.

Mr. Fletcher turned out to be an insane-looking scrawny old man in a night gown standing on the balcony of the second floor of the housing unit adjacent to Nathan's own. What made Mr. Fletcher look insane was the rather large pump-action shotgun he was holding, and the spent cartridges that littered the floor of his balcony. Mr. Fletcher had found out about the post-fabrication plan and responded to it with some annoyance, shooting at the post-fabricators who had arrived to drive them off. In so doing, he'd discovered he rather liked the whole yelling and shooting at people from the balcony bit, and resolved to start doing it regularly. These days he shot at teenagers, birds, plumbers, salesmen, tourists, and anyone else who he felt didn't belong on the street.

At the moment he was leveling his rather deadly looking shotgun at a group of salesmen who he suspected were up to no good, on the excellent grounds that they were salesmen, and young whippersnappers, and that they were wearing clothes that he did not recognize. Several loud shots rang out as he fired at them. A group of a half dozen or so had taken cover behind a large sturdy fence on the edge of Mr. Fletcher's property.

"Perhaps," one of the salesmen shouted out, "you would like to consider an installment plan."

The load of buckshot that Mr. Fletcher sent towards him by way of response pinged musically off of the xylophone fence.

"Zero down payment," shouted another, before Mr. Fletcher sent a second spread of shot flying over his head.

"Get off of my property," Fletcher spat at them.

Brian stared.

"Hello, Mr. Fletcher," Nathan called out genially as he sauntered towards the mailbox.

"Oh, hello Nathan," Fletcher croaked, his eyes only briefly leaving the sights of his shotgun to observe his neighbor.

"What's the count for today?" Nathan asked genially.

"I've fired forty-six shells and hit three whippersnappers, six salesmen, a cyclist, and the mailman," Fletcher said. "A few teenagers also came by, but I let them get away."

"Mmm..." Nathan hummed, as if this were completely normal. He opened his mailbox to discover it was empty. "Still no delivery? It's getting late."

"The mail service is getting worse and worse around here," Fletcher agreed, amid a cacophony of shots aimed at the salesman.

Brian was too stunned and terrified to say anything, but his eyes fell on the abandoned mailtruck on the opposite side of the street. It was on fire, peppered with bullet holes.

One of the salesman apparently thought the discussion of mail service constituted an opening for his sales pitch, as he shouted, "subscribe now for free shipping and handling!" He ducked back behind the fence to avoid Mr. Fletcher's reply.

"Who's your friend?" Mr. Fletcher asked, glancing at Brian.

"Didn't you see him come in?"

"I saw a policeman come in," Mr. Fletcher replied, "but you know I don't like to bother your guests."

"He is not a policeman," Nathan explained. "He is a bureaucrat trying to get me to sign a form."

"Terrible nuisance, paperwork," Mr. Fletcher said.

"Satisfaction guaranteed or your money-"

There was a loud bang, and the salesman finished his pitch with a sound like "urgle burgle."

"It's absolutely necessary," Brian said mechanically.

Fletcher held up a cautioning hand. "Excuse me for one moment." He reached into the pocket of his night gown and pulled out what looked to be a grenade, and threw it - with surprising accuracy for a man of his age - behind the fence. The salesmen scampered out from behind the fence and then dropped as Fletcher picked them off.

"I am very unhappy about the mail service though," he said as he did this. "I had a letter for pick up."

"Did you?" Nathan asked.

"Oh yes. It was a donation for the local chapter of the International Committee of the Red Cross. I make a sizable contribution every year."

"Why?"

"I suppose," said Fletcher, as he sighted another salesman, "I am just a pacifist at heart."

There was a loud bang as he brought down the final salesman.

"Are you aware that you are creating rather a lot of paperwork for other people?" Brian asked him, eyeing the bodies of the salesmen. "By killing them, I mean."

"Oh, don't worry sonny. They're not dead. They're just stunned."

Brian did not think that stunned people tended to produce quite so much blood.

"Stunned are they?"

"Yes. I fire rubber bullets." Fletcher broke into a wicked grin. "Sometimes."

Nathan, meanwhile, had picked up the newspaper from his driveway that he had apparently neglected to fetch earlier in the day. It was mostly drawn in crayon, though the illustrations were done in magic marker.

Fletcher, apparently satisfied that the salesmen were adequately stunned, ducked back into his home to reload. Nathan, whistling, tucked his paper under one arm and returned to his home. Brian turned to follow him, but as he turned, he saw another salesman sneaking out from behind a nearby hedge and maneuvering back towards Fletcher's home.

Brian caught the man by the arm.

"Did you see what just happened? You don't seriously mean to go back, do you?"

"No, no, it's alright," the salesman said excitedly. "I sell shotgun shells."

Brian looked after him in disbelief for a moment, then ducked back into Nathan's house.

"Does that happen every day?" he asked Nathan.

"More or less," Nathan affirmed.

Brian slumped down into one of Nathan's green chairs in disbelief.

"And you live here?"

"I've lived here all my life."

"How do you stand it?"

"Stand what?" Nathan asked, turning to the next page of his paper, which was just one constant waxy crayon squiggle.

"Well, the threat of death, for one thing."

"I have a brain lesion-"

"Let me rephrase the question. How does your family put up with it?"

"All of my family died, I'm afraid," Nathan said.

"That doesn't surprise me in the slightest - but I meant, why did they come to Dead Donkey in the first place?"

"Oh, I don't know. But my family has lived here for generations."

Brian goggled at him.

Nathan's family had in fact lived in Dead Donkey for generations. Nathan had been raised by his father; his mother left before he was born. Nathan's father worked in the xylophone factory, and earned an honest and musical living until the factory burned down, and he had subsequently choked on a hard candy that he mistook for a soft candy. His aunt had been a zookeeper at the Dead Donkey zoo, until it transpired that there was no Dead Donkey zoo, as the animals that the zookeepers had hitherto thought were being kept in transparent animal enclosures were in fact just being polite. The Dead Donkey Zoo's board of trustees insists it has now rectified this small oversight by constructing transparent animal enclosures. If so no one is entirely sure where these enclosures might be, because they are certainly not enclosing the animals.

The better liked of Nathan's two grandfathers had been a very well respected local magician. His immensely popular signature act consisted of walking through a solid wall, and although his technique for doing so involved a sledge and a chainsaw, it still drew crowds so tremendous that he had once been responsible for the Great Dead Donkey Theater Floor Collapse. Unfortunately, his wizard-grandfather had eventually been killed by a faulty bathtub. His death so outraged the public that they formed a lynch mob to hunt down and string up the perpetrator.

While Nathan's grandfather had been the best known member of the family, his other relatives were also quite distinguished. Nathan's grandmother had been a treasure hunter. She maintained throughout her life that she had discovered ancient documents proving that there was hidden gold in the city and insisted Captain Kidd buried his treasure in Dead Donkey. Why Captain Kidd would have buried his treasure in Dead Donkey, which was three hundred miles inland from entirely the wrong ocean, remained a mystery. Nathan's other grandmother had been a social engineer, and had managed to dramatically reduce poverty and wealth inequality in the city of Dead Donkey by introducing the concept of armed robbery to the masses. She was later crushed to death by a life support machine.

Nathan's other grandfather had been a faulty bathtub manufacturer, and had been lynched by an angry mob when he was found out.

Nathan's third grandfather had been a firefighterfighter, which is to say he worked closely with the arsonists. He'd gone out in a blaze of glory. He remains a legend in the city's firefighterfighter community, and the arsonists continue to light eternal flames in tribute to him (or so they claim).

Brian listened to Nathan tell him all this. The latter concluded his story by saying:

"I am very proud of my family."

Brian was speechless.

"What about *your* family?" Nathan asked Brian.

"I don't like to talk about my family."

"Why not?"

"I don't like to talk about talking about my family either."

"Why not?"

"I just don't."

Nathan considered.

"Perhaps you could do some kind of interpretive dance." He looked dead serious.

Brian was about to deliver some sort of biting remark about dancing on Nathan's little toe when the phone rang. Nathan picked it up.

"Hello," he said.

There was a pause.

"Oh, yes. You can come right over." He put down the phone. "Excuse me," he said to Brian. "I am expecting company and I have to get ready."

Nathan stood and walked out of the room, then returned with a plate of little snack cakes and pitcher of coffee. No sooner had he done this than the doorbell rang. Nathan went over and answered it.

A man with a very broad smile was standing on the doorstep. He shook Nathan's hand in a jaunty handshake.

"So good to see you again!" he said cheerily.

"And you," Nathan said with equal cheeriness. "Come in, come in. What can I do for you?"

"I wouldn't have believed it myself but it looks like you're back again. We'll just have to do something about that, won't we? Oh, and you have company! How silly of me. I didn't mean to intrude."

"You're not intruding. He was just leaving."

"I was not," Brian said insistently.

The grinning man took another one of Nathan's several green chairs and sat down in it. He stretched his legs in a leisurely manner.

"Can I offer you some coffee?" Nathan asked.

"I would but I really shouldn't drink anything while I'm working. It could lead to... some unnecessary complications," the grinning man finished.

Nathan poured him a cup anyway and seized one of the snack cakes.

The smiling man ignored this, but hung his head apologetically.

"I am terribly sorry for my tardiness. I would have come earlier but there is a very strange old man who lives next door to you-"

"Don't mind Mr. Fletcher. He won't hurt you unless you try to sell him something or walk on his grass. What brings you back here?"

"I heard the funniest rumor that you had come back, and you know I wouldn't have believed it myself. One does encounter the funniest problems in this business... but you know, if word got out that I had come to visit you, but you were still... around, so to speak, that could be very bad for my reputation. Very bad indeed. So we'll just have to take care of it. Nothing personal, of course, Mr. Haynes. Just part of my work."

Brian was getting the impression that there was something very strange going on here. He straightened his tie.

"What do you do exactly?"

"I am a serial killer," the grinning man said quietly. And before Brian could react, he drew a silenced pistol out of his pocket and shot Brian dead.

Nathan sipped his coffee and looked bemusedly at Brian for a second or so, until the serial killer shot him too, and then the world went black.

A mechanical woman's voice sounded out.

"Station number four, please."

Suddenly, Nathan was standing in line behind rather a lot of salesman who had not, in fact, been stunned. The frumpy woman at the desk looked up and spotted him.

"You again?" she demanded irritably.

Chapter 9

Reality has an odd sense of humor. The evidence for this is everywhere, from the duck-billed platypus to the warning tags on mattresses to the as-yet-undiscovered Sinistra hagfish, a deep-sea fish that only has one eye and only believes in the existence of the world to the left of itself and not right, and therefore spends its whole life going in circles, much like a lot of people. But Sinistra hagfish aside, nowhere is this sense of humor so apparent as in the city of Dead Donkey.

For example, consider the case of Christopher Seidel, a lifelong Dead Donkey resident who has been hailed as the blindest man alive. Seidel earned this title not because he was totally blind (which a good many people are), but rather because he absolutely insisted that he could see, though he absolutely, definitely could not. He eschewed the usual aids of a cane, guide dog, and dark glasses and instead went around bumping into hydrants and fences and staging loud, one-sided conversations with nearby lamp posts about the weather, much to the bemusement of passersby. When people pointed out to him that he couldn't see, Seidel would furiously deny the simple fact and attempt to describe his surroundings in great detail, which would inevitably come out as a description of Time Square in New York, since he couldn't see them. Hence, he was not only blind but also blind to his own blindness, and therefore the blindest man alive.

One particular morning, after Seidel had quite happily put on his polka-dot-feather gown and pink women's tennis shoes and shaved while monitoring his reflection in a bathroom Salvador Dali painting, he tripped over a diamond which - by complete coincidence - had been unearthed by a good-natured squirrel and deposited on his front steps. This diamond was so magnificently, incredibly, jawdroppingly large and beautiful that could they have but seen it, DeBeers' top executives would have given up the diamond trade on the spot. The curator of the Smithsonian Museum of Natural History would have thrown the Hope Diamond into the trash, cursing at it for the time and space it had wasted during its tenure, and Marilyn Monroe would have made a credible effort at time travel to get her hands on it.

Seidel would have wept for joy. As it happened, though, he couldn't see it, but Seidel was convinced he had found a large and inconveniently placed rock. He took it inside and used it as a paperweight for his important papers (which were actually takeout menus that he believed to be tax returns). It will, consequently, never be seen by human eyes, although the squirrel will occasionally come back to visit it.

Another example is the case of little ten-year-old Jimmy Millican, a young schoolboy enrolled in Dead Donkey elementary school, who spent a few of his mornings in math class learning about prime numbers. (Some aspects of the Dead Donkey education system will be discussed in greater depth in later chapters.) In between doodles of space ships and what the school psychiatrist would later generously label "water gun fights," Jimmy Millican would happen to devise and scribble down a perfectly general method of quickly and easily finding the prime factorization of any number, no matter how large. He assumed this to be totally unimportant, and quite frankly boring.

In fact this was so mindbendingly important that if anyone had known about it, every intelligence officer, covert operative, secret service agent, codebreaker, code-unbreaker, spook, ghost, ghoul, and CIA janitor would have swooped down on Jimmy where he sat, only to be shoved out of the way by a horde of angry number theorists loudly proclaiming that it couldn't possibly be right, only for the number theorists to be themselves trampled by the rampaging Fields Medal committee in their rush to give Jimmy this and several other distinguished awards.

As it happened though, the only person who ever saw this was Jimmy's math teacher and subsequently the school psychiatrist, who decided that the most important thing on the page was in fact the doodling of the "water gun fights" with his fellow classmates. Jimmy would subsequently be transferred to a special class and go on to work as a professional speed bump.

But such is life.

Chapter 10

After a few minutes of waiting and a certain amount of shouting, Nathan found himself back in Director Fulcher's office. Fulcher was stalking back and forth like a panther that had just been fired from an accounting job. The look in his eye was murderous.

"So." He said to Nathan. "So."

Brian was in the seat next to Nathan. He shifted uncomfortably.

Nathan stared benignly back at Fulcher.

"So?" Nathan prompted querulously.

"I decided to have a look at your file," Fulcher said, "to find out why you are such a troublesome man. Would you like to see your file, Mr. Haynes?"

"I suppose so," Nathan said.

"Here is your file."

Fulcher opened an impossibly deep drawer in his desk and out of this impossibly deep drawer he drew an impossibly large file, a file so large that the room had to dramatically expand to house it. Space wobbled nauseously and inconveniently around them, twisting and yawning as the room inflated. By the end of it, the file was about the size of a small house, and inside it were about a quizillion forms written in unreadably small print. Their tops all said things like, "Form 16573: Authorization to Have a Dream About Frogs.", "Form 87103: Certification That Subject Has Never Interacted With Mr. Travis Erwin Habsworth, of 2388 Shillington Road, Albany," and "Form 000-0: This is not a Form."

Nathan blinked at it a bit bashfully. He guessed he had never realized how much paperwork he caused for other people.

"Is my social security number somewhere in there?" he asked pleasantly. "It's just that I've forgotten my social security number, so if you could tell me what it is-"

"Everything that you have ever done is in here," Fulcher said dryly.

"It's just that I think my social security number is terribly important for something. I think I have to use it to-"

"To fill out forms?" Director Fulcher asked, one eyebrow raised.

"Oh yes, I guess so."

"I happened across your 19247-O," Fulcher continued. As he spoke, a particular form zoomed out of the pile and onto his desk. The heading read, "Form 19247-O: Notice of Behaviors That Represent A Viable Threat To Oneself And Others."

"It says here that you failed to regard an armed serial killer as a threat to either yourself or Mr. Dithershoes."

"Well, it wasn't as if he was a stranger. He was a serial killer I knew."

"It says you let him kill you."

"Yes."

"Twice."

"He asked very politely, so I didn't really see why I shouldn't."

Fulcher bridged his knobby fingers and regarded Nathan imperiously.

"You are completely insane."

"Oh good," Nathan said cheerily. "I was beginning to worry that reality was insane, but if it's just me then that's alright."

"You are completely insane," Fulcher repeated, "and I have

nstructed my subordinates to add a note to that effect in your file."

"Isn't that what this is?" Nathan said looking confusedly at the 19247-O.

"No. This merely says that you are dangerous. The process to have you flagged as insane involves somewhat more paperwork."

"Oh, I'm terribly sorry about that."

"Once you are flagged as insane, I will not need you to sign your 21B anymore. It will be signed without you."

"What?" Nathan yelled, jumping out of his chair.

"Yes. I shall be able to sign on your behalf," Director Fulcher said with a grim smile. "And that will be the end of this little game of ours."

"Are we playing a game?" Nathan asked confusedly. "Do you have Monopoly?"

"I have the monopoly on your future," Fulcher said.

"Is that a variant? What are the rules?"

"Never mind. I still cannot have you here until the paperwork is prepared, so I will send you back in the meantime."

Fulcher reached into his desk and produced a new form.

"Mr. Dithershoes, you will go back with him to keep an eye on him."

Brian sat up very straight.

"Yes, Director Fulcher."

Fulcher signed the form before him, and the world winked out of existence again.

Chapter 11

Misdirection is a handy tool for anyone who wants to direct attention away from his mistakes. It has been used to great effect by certain Presidential administrations, which have cleverly used the war to distract from the abysmal state of the economy, and simultaneously cleverly used the economy to distract from the abysmal state of the war. Misdirection is also commonly employed by petty shoplifters in convenience stores, who shrewdly attempt to direct attention away from the things they are haphazardly shoving into their bags by waving a gun around in the air and declaring that they are robbing the store. The trick, you see, is too keep attention on the gun and no one will notice the theft. (This is, by coincidence, exactly the same technique as used by the Presidential administrations, only on a smaller scale.)

Hannibal, the famous Carthaginian General, employed misdirection against the Roman Consul Sempronius Longus at the Battle of Trebia by approaching his enemies while looking up on horseback and then loudly engaging them in conversation about the weather, commenting about the unseasonable warmth for this time of year and how he hoped it didn't turn into rain some other time because he had this big battle he was hoping to fight. The Romans looked up and were subsequently so preoccupied by the weather that they didn't notice Hannibal killing them. For this outstanding victory, Hannibal is remembered as the father of strategy, but in truth, he is not its first practitioner.

The bureaucrats who run reality are masters of misdirection. They would like us to believe they are infallible, and will go to great lengths to maintain the illusion, but the truth is that they aren't. Take, for example, the case of the Great Superbath of Latifia.

The Great Superbath of Latifia was one of the most incredible wonders of the ancient world. It was larger than the mightiest of the legendary Pyramids at Giza, involved more inspired ancient engineering than the Hanging Gardens of Babylon, and provided much more comfort and entertainment to the masses than the Coliseum at Rome.

In addition to having taken one-hundred-and-fifty million consecutive Sunday afternoons by one-hundred-and-fifty thousand eager Latifian bathers to build, as part of a laborious and (it must be said) immensely stupid building process that involved rolling the tiny pebbles that made up the bath one rock at a time from a quarry five hundred miles away when there was a much more convenient one just down the road, it required an immense amount of paperwork on the parts of the cosmic bureaucrats to maintain. There was the Form 8183982 - Notice of Continued Existence of A Giant Bath - to consider, not to mention the Form 260821 - Declaration of an Element of the Common Heritage of Mankind - but also - and this was the part that really left the cosmic bureaucrats gritting their teeth - the Form 6236091 - Co-Bathing Postulation, which was a form that had to be filled out for every person already in the bath whenever another person entered it. While this was all fine and dandy for a simple bath, or a mother bathing her daughter, or a man bathing his gazelle, it was a ridiculous amount of paperwork for the bureaucrats to file when the entirety of the Latifian civilization hopped into the Great Superbath together, then proceeded to get in and out all the time whenever they remembered they had something they needed to do to maintain the civilization.

The number of forms that needed to be filled out, which

started out at just a total of one for the second person and three for the third person and six for the fourth person soon ballooned to a quizillion, and was further complicated by the Latifian "Let's all get into and out of the bath in sequence day."

Ultimately, despite their incredibly great and much-lauded efficiency, the cosmic bureaucrats were not able to keep their papers in order, and they misfiled a 6236091 as a 6236091A - Form to Enable Someone To Dig Out Their Earwax With A Twig. The result was that all of a sudden the Latifian bath simply ceased to be. All its vast, great pipes and the main aqueducts that it had taken to supply it, the super-water-heaters and the giant megafires, the towering walls and the ultrawaterslides, all vanished in a heartbeat.

What was left after the screw-up was resolved was a whole lot of very confused bathers who were suddenly sitting on the hard ground.

The bureaucrats were mortified and immediately began to conceal their mistake by erasing every single bit of the Great Superbaths of Latifia in the historical record, the geological record, the archaeological record, and from human understanding generally. The problem was that the Latifians were walking around telling everyone about how they'd used to have a nice, warm giant superbath that had suddenly disappeared and were generally believed, so after a while the bureaucrats decided they would simply have to do something about the Latifians too and made them all disappear as well. When all the people of classical Europe then began to wonder aloud what had ever happened to the Latifians - the strange but wholly pleasant and affable people who had always seemed to have bathing suits available and invented the rubber ducky before the iron sword, the cosmic bureaucrats decided there was simply nothing else for it and made the entire Latifian homeland disappear. This very effectively distracted everyone from the problem of where the baths had gone since the whole of Latifia had vanished, and is hence a masterstroke in misdirection.

Over time, the Europeans came to assume that it had been some kind of crazy myth and mostly forgot about Latifia, which we now call Atlantis, though the cultural memories of their vast bath and rubber duckies live on in the stories of their great technological and moral superiority.

The whole incident sparked an internal review of the bath form filing procedures, the results of which are still pending on the bureaucratic side, and should become available in another 6-to-8 thousand years, though of course delays are possible as thoroughness cannot be sacrificed for the sake of expediency. Since the incident, the bureaucrat responsible has been placed on paid leave, although he has never been able to collect any of the pay he is due because he is still filling out the immensely complicated Form 6624605 - Assessment of the Results of Destroying a Giant Bath Due to Filing Error, and more recently a 1193035 - Explanation of Delay in Filing Bath-Related Assessment.

Despite the pending review, the bureaucrats were left with a sense of animosity towards giant baths in all their forms after the Latifians disappeared, as the embarrassment of the incident lingers with them. They have subsequently worked to covertly sabotage all giant bath-related projects worldwide, which is the real reason the Roman Empire collapsed. It is also the reason that modern baths require something called grouting, which apparently no other fixture in the house even occasionally requires.

The point is that bureaucrats don't like making mistakes,

even though they sometimes do, and they don't like to be made to feel foolish, even though they sometimes are. Nathan Haynes, with his brain damage and his stubborn refusal to put his papers in order, made Director Fulcher and his subordinates feel foolish and - in practical terms - represented a mistake on their part. That's why they intended to try so very hard to get Nathan to sign his 21B even if he didn't want to. Practically speaking, there is nothing more abhorrent to a bureaucrat than an unsigned form, except perhaps for a giant bath.

Chapter 12

Brian stumbled back and forth a little as he rematerialized in the living world.

Nathan was looking at his living room with his arms crossed. Both of their previous bodies were laying dead on the floor. He stared at them for a few seconds, then announced, "I have just remembered that I have forgotten to do my laundry."

He walked off. Brian stared after him. A washing machine roared to life somewhere down the hall, then Nathan returned, his arms still crossed.

"My living room is getting very messy," he said unhappily. "I don't suppose you know a good carpet cleaner?"

"No," Brian answered.

"Oh dear," Nathan said, and walked over to the phone. He picked it up off the receiver and dialed three numbers.

"Hello?" started Nathan. "Yes, I would like to report that I have been murdered again. Just now. Yes- Hello? Hello?" He put the receiver back in its cradle.

"They hung up," he explained with disappointment.

"I can't imagine why," Brian said sarcastically.

"Hold that thought," Nathan interrupted cheerily. "I've just thought of someone else I could call." He picked the phone back up and dialed some more numbers. "Hello? Guinness Book? I would like to apply for the record of the most number of times anyone has ever been murdered. I have been murdered twice."

There was a pause.

"What do you mean you don't take that sort of record? No one has been murdered more, have they? And I wonder if you could recommend a good carpet cleaning service. The blood on my... hello? Hello?"

He put down the receiver again.

"They hung up as well," Nathan said unhappily. He looked around the living room. "Well, help me put these bodies outside. You take yours."

They both dragged their bodies outside and piled them onto the wheelbarrow, on top of Nathan's first body.

As they did this, Brian could not help but ask a question.

"Why did you let him murder us?"

"I make it a point to support the city's murderer community," Nathan said airily. The murderers were by far the most dynamic criminals in the city ever since the muggers unionized.

"You are insane," Brian reported, on returning to Nathan's living room.

Nathan thought about this as he sat down in one of his green chairs and reflected on the events of the past few hours. "What did Director Fulcher mean about declaring me insane?"

"Well, if he fills out the appropriate paperwork, he can have you declared insane, meaning you aren't competent to decide things for yourself. Then he doesn't need you to sign forms anymore. He can sign them himself."

"That doesn't seem entirely fair," Nathan said with a frown.

"We can't have a load of insane people running around doing... everything you've done so far today, basically."

"I haven't really done anything today," Nathan argued. "I haven't even finished doing the laundry."

Brian emitted an exasperated sigh.

"It doesn't really matter, I guess. We can just wait for the Director to finish filling out the paperwork. Then it will all be over. The next time you die, you'll have to stay dead."

"I can't have that," Nathan said with a frown. "What if I got a form from my doctor saying that I'm not insane?"

"That would be strong evidence your doctor is insane as well."

Nathan considered this. "No, I think he's alright. We should go see him." He stood up, and before Brian realized what he was doing, Nathan had walked out the door.

Brian followed him out into the yard only to see Nathan apparently stealing his neighbor's car.

"What-?" Brian started.

"I'm just borrowing it," Nathan assured him as he stuck what appeared to be a slim jim down the driver-side window. "My neighbor on this side is Mr. Chamness. He doesn't drive very much."

Mr. Chamness didn't drive very much partially because he wasn't a very good driver, but also because he was blind. He'd therefore told Nathan he could feel free to break into the car and use it whenever he liked, provided that Nathan did a few odd jobs for him, like watering his cat and changing his plants' litter boxes.

After a few seconds, Nathan had defeated the anti-theft mechanisms, silenced the car alarm, and slid into the driver's seat. Brian got into the passenger side.

"Are we going to the hospital?" Brian asked as Nathan hotwired the ignition.

"No," Nathan said cheerily. "My doctor is at the university. The hospital closed recently."

"Oh. Why is that?"

"It turned out it was full of sick people."

Brian resolved to spend the rest of the journey in silence. His resolution was severely challenged at the first traffic intersection. While there were a number of peculiar things about this intersection, it wasn't the fact that the lights were colored purple and pink rather than red or green that surprised him. Neither was it the twisted and rickety, and frankly dangerous-looking architectures that flanked the street. Rather, it was the young man surrounded by a group of thugs on the street corner, being beaten with unpleasant looking sticks.

The thugs patted the young man down.

"Is he being mugged?" Brian exclaimed as he watched through the window.

"No, just playing Muleball," the young man called back. "Not to worry."

Nathan drove on, and Brian returned to stunned silence.

At the next traffic light, there was a man sitting on the street corner in what appeared to be a stolen child's lemonade stand, with the colorful words "Lemonade" crossed out and replaced with "Bank" in equally colorful letters. A rather large and terrifying looking black man with several ear piercings was sitting behind the counter. His account register was, on closer inspection, a children's coloring book. On occasion, as people walked in front of him, he would yell, "Give me your money!" in an extremely insistent way and usually, they did.

"Who's that?" Brian asked, looking apprehensively at the man.

"That's Jermaine," Nathan replied cheerily. "He runs the bank."

Although it would have taken an extremely shrewd observer to realize it, Jermaine was not actually a banker. His shop was not a bank. In fact, the flimsy particleboard was a clever ruse to deceive the unwary into thinking he was a banker, leading them to surrender their money to him. Jermaine himself was a highly successful con artist.

Most people in Dead Donkey had long since realized this, of course, but they continued to bank with him primarily because he was consistently able to deliver a higher rate of return than most commercial banks, and because of his excellent customer service.

"I think banks are usually a bit more formal," Brian said uncertainly. "I'm fairly sure they're supposed to have offices and forms and things."

"We don't put up with that kind of bureaucracy in Dead Donkey." They drove for a little while longer. "He also offers insurance policies," Nathan added as they went.

"Does he - er - do much insurance business?"

"No. Sadly, all the valuations for our properties here are negative."

This deeply unsettled Brian. He was a bureaucrat, and this chaos and informality that whipped around the city of Dead Donkey like a cold wind through the Eastern Front rattled him deeply. He looked around for something familiar, and his eyes came to rest on a man carrying a large set of books and binders in his arms as he walked down the street. Brian found it somehow calming to watch this man for a while, as he was able to assure himself that the binders contained paperwork, and therefore some semblance of the things Brian was accustomed to.

In fact, this person was the only man alive who went into restaurants to ask to see the government-mandated health inspector's reports. He did this because many restaurants - particularly in Dead Donkey - did not have these like they were supposed to and would occasionally offer him bribes or free food to keep him quiet. Brian probably would have been quite troubled if he'd known this, because one of the laws of the universe that he as a bureaucrat was sworn to enforce was that there's no such thing as a free lunch, and if you have ever received a free lunch, karma is bound to turn around and get you sooner or later. (Generally, 'sooner or later,' is when the karma desk clears its backlog and files the appropriate 68240A: Instrument of Lunch-Related Retribution.) By coincidence, in the case of this particular man, this karmic redress came exactly as Nathan turned the corner and plunged the man out of sight, at which point he was attacked by a migrating flock of angry geese, who subsequently seized his wallet and took it upon themselves to destroy his credit rating.

However, Brian never knew or saw any of this, and was much happier for it.

After another block, where the only peculiarity that Brian saw was an advertisement for a Weight Loss Fork (now including a free Weight Loss Spoon with every purchase; safely destroys your soup before you can drink it), Nathan pulled up to the side of the road and parked. He got out and went up to the nearest of the nearby parking meters and pressed a button on it. It ejected eight quarters, which Nathan took from the coin return, and flashed the message "thank you for parking here!" on its electronic screen. Brian stared at it.

As they walked down the street towards (Brian assumed) the university, an impeccably dressed man rounded the corner in front of them. He rapidly walked up to them and held out some pamphlets for them to take.

"Hello," he said brightly. "I'd like to talk to you about atheism."

"Not today, thanks," Nathan said.

"There is no God and life is a series of meaningless

tragedies," the atheist replied cheerily.

The man went away but had somehow managed to push a pamphlet into Brian's hands. It read, "Church of Particularly Cynical Atheism, Services Friday, Saturday, Sunday, English, Spanish, Urdu..."

Brian shoved it into his pocket.

"They have been having a turf war with the Church of Atheist Absolutists," Nathan said matter-of-factly.

"You have two atheist churches in the city?"

"No. We have one atheist church. The members of the Church of Atheist Absolutists do not believe the church exists."

"Ahh..."

They continued down the street. Looking up, Brian could see a very tall, stately building in the distance that was much more eye-pleasing than the rest of the vomit-colored monstrosities around him. It seemed to be getting closer.

"Is that where we're going?"

"Yes. That's the university's spire. It's the tallest building in the city."

"How tall is it?"

"Oh, twice as tall as something and more than half as tall as something else."

"Very impressive."

The university's gate was only a block or so distant now. As they approached it, they passed a group of masked men with a rather large array of rifles slung over their shoulders and a picture of a slightly blurry dot on the backs of their shirts. Brian was sure he had seen the blurry dot before, but the significance did not come to him. The masked men had a video camera, and they were actively filming the side of the building, where they had lined up a large array of clothes mannequins and one terrified looking young man.

"Let's wait for them to finish," Nathan whispered.

"Who are they?" Brian hissed back.

"They're the PLF - the Pluto Liberation Front."

Brian suddenly realized what the little dot on the back of their shirts was.

One of the men, apparently the leader, was now standing in front of the camera, brandishing his rifle in the air and shouting, "we will execute one hostage an hour until Pluto is restored to its rightful planetary status!"

All of the men around him gave a huge cry of exultation, and the one man on the side of the building whimpered.

The camera shut off. The leader turned to Nathan and Brian and winked at them.

"Don't worry," he said. "They're only mannequins."

"I told you I'm not a mannequin!" the terrified young man shouted.

"Oh yes you are," the leader said, frowning at him. "I've been fooled by mannequins before. I'm not making that mistake again."

Nathan nudged Brian.

"We'd better move on."

They started to walk away quickly.

"But that man-"

"Quickly, before they decide you're a mannequin too."

Chapter 13

They reached the gates of the university, where a green field and a handful of distant building complexes spread out. Several perfectly normal-looking students with bags slung over their shoulders chatted merrily and walked past them. The cries of the PLF faded into the background as Nathan - who apparently knew exactly where they were going - walked into one of the buildings. Written on the side were the words "The Dead Donkey Milton Prodmany Center For Biological and Biomedical Sciences."

Nathan stopped in front of a large list of locations within the building posted in the lobby. He peered at it. Brian, meanwhile, was left looking at the bust of an insane-looking man labelled "Milton Prodmany." Prodmany was grinning broadly but only had two teeth, and what appeared to be an iguana was chewing on his hair.

"It says here that Neurosciences - that's where we'll find my doctor - is right next to Molecular Biology." Nathan tapped the shoulder of a passing researcher to stop her. "Excuse me - which way is Molecular Biology?"

The researcher chuckled.

"That's a good one," she said. "Very funny," and walked away without further explanation.

It should be explained for readers who might not know that many people assume large tracts of science like evolutionary biology, immunology, climatology, etc., must be fake. In fact, these scientific disciplines are all completely factual, and evolution, vaccines, and climate change respectively are verifiably real and/or efficacious.

However, there is no such scientific discipline as molecular biology. In much the same way that Jermaine the banker is actually a con artist, molecular biology is in fact a scam for grant money. It is a marvelous scam, a scam in which a man in a white lab coat calling himself a molecular biologist could write a paper riddled with completely nonsensical mumbo-jumbo like "DNAzymes Autocatalyze Genome Replication Through Irregular Hairpin Motifs.' Then later the men in labcoats would announce that eating too many bananas causes acne or something, and then people would simply throw money at them based on the presumption that it was incredibly important, while the men in lab coats claimed they could predict your acne based on banana intake.

This is of course totally different from being a psychic. Psychics wear turbans and rarely, if ever, mention proteins.

People claiming to be molecular biologists are (much like Jermaine) con artists, who are supplying the public's insane demands for a never-ending list of highly technical reasons that their butts look big and they can't stop eating cake and whatnot. They spend most of their days playing tetris, and write three or four papers a year - these days mostly produced by computerized random word generators plus random insertions of the words "motif" and "protein", with the addition of an internal competition to see who can get away with the silliest name for something - then reap huge paychecks. Then they all buy subscriptions to each others' journals on the university's dime and go laughing all the way to the bank (Jermaine).

The only other two scientific fields that are scams are cosmology and deep sea oceanography.

Cosmology is basically the study of objects that are too far away to see (astronomy being the study of things that are close enough to see). It is therefore by definition impossible for cosmologists to discover anything, because they can't see them, and if they do see them it instantly becomes astronomy and is no longer their problem. While the cosmologists did try to research the universe for a few decades, after a while they were forced to admit that they didn't really understand anything and the universe was incredibly huge and terrifying and they couldn't identify the vast majority of the things in it. Most cosmologists now spend the bulk of their time arguing with astrologers (who are part of the aforementioned turban-wearing class of people) and producing TV documentaries about the universe. This is also why most discoveries in cosmology are now made by a single wheelchair-bound man who has great difficulty looking up unassisted. Thanks to him we now know that the universe started with a bang but it all pretty much went downhill from there.

Deep sea oceanography is the other scientific discipline that is complete nonsense. It is the study of the ocean and consists, mainly, of sitting in unimaginably small submarines at depths that are not quite deep enough to crush them into even smaller tin cans. It is a complete waste of time. The deep ocean is mostly empty, and those parts that are not empty are exclusively filled with things like the previously mentioned and as-yet undiscovered Sinistra hagfish, which are all at the same time ugly, stupid, and totally irrelevant to the proceedings of science. The field of deep sea oceanography was invented by claustrophiliacs (people who enjoy being confined in small spaces, the opposite of claustrophobics) and people who are willing to go to particularly extreme lengths for some peace and quiet.

Arctic exploration used to be the fourth quasi-scientific

discipline that was a total scam, but it is now defunct. Arctic explorers never really wanted to explore the arctic and in fact only ever discovered what they knew before they started: that the arctic is cold, lonely, and desolate. The field began as an attempt to engineer a circumstance in which it is socially acceptable to consume sled dogs. They succeeded, but due to lack of interest and growing public demands to know what happened to all the sled dogs there used to be running around all over the place, the relevant institutions hastily disbanded and happily no longer exist.

Brian and Nathan didn't know any of this. They still believed that molecular biology was a real science, and were therefore left baffled when the young woman they had just spoken to started to giggle uncontrollably at a nearby bulletin board. The bulletin board announced that the molecular biology lab had published a new paper "Hoaxer Ilyushin Protein Shishkekabs Malachite Poetry Complex."

Nathan calmly stepped over the laughing woman and began to walk down the hallway.

"Do you know where we're going?" Brian asked him.

"Let us say, for the sake of argument, that I do."

This answer somehow rattled Brian even more than a no. They were going deeper and deeper into the laboratory complex and the air seemed to be getting colder. The stark concrete walls seemed to be closing in on them, and the distant animal squeaks grew more distinct and louder. A room full of lab rats and researchers came into view. The dumb creatures scurried around, unsuccessfully navigating the maze before them, sniffing the odd bit of cheese at the end of one corridor or another, before occasionally settling down and taking a measurement of the rats' behavior.

Brian was quite sure that they were going in the wrong direction. In point of fact, they were going in the right direction, though, and a few minutes later they passed a sign that said, "Molecular Biology Department and Broom Closet," which told them they were on the right track. It regarded them in silent, judgmental contempt as they passed it.

"And is there any point in my asking why your doctor works in a laboratory?"

"I am told that my condition is quite unusual and is worthy of research."

"What have they found about your condition?"

"I think they have discovered that I'm not quite right."

"Someone had better get the nobel prize committee on the phone," Brian said sarcastically.

They stopped in front of a large room with the words, "Neurobiology," written across it. Nathan knocked and entered. No sooner had he done so than a large white blur bounded up to Nathan and started shaking his hand.

This white blur was Nathan's doctor, a middle-aged research scientist and doctor named Dr. Irving Vegatillius. He was short with dark eyes and was obviously going bald.

Like all scientists he was wearing a lab coat to display his seriousness. It is a little known trade secret in science, but all scientists except oceanographers, arctic explorers, cosmologists, and molecular biologists wear white lab coats. This is a handy way to tell their disciplines apart from the rest of science, and is in fact how funding authorities differentiate between real scientists and one of the aforementioned four disciplines. Never tell an oceanographer, arctic explorer, cosmologist, or molecular biologist this simple fact or the entire foundation of science will come crashing down and subsequently send the human quest for understanding into considerable disarray. If you ever see a molecular biologist wearing a lab coat, you should alert the authorities immediately and, as an interim measure, spill ink or paint onto their coat to render it less white and claim it was an accident.

In addition to his lab coat, Dr. Vegatillius was wearing a very silly hat. This hat was of no further significance whatsoever, but owing to its large size, irregular shape, brightly colored pink feathers, and rainbow rim, it did rather undermine the respectability of the lab coat. While I will not bring it up again, note that the impact of the silly hat underpinned the rest of the encounter.

"Absolutely wonderful to see you again," Dr. Vegatillius exclaimed, shaking Nathan's hand like he was panning for gold in his knuckles.

"Good to see you again too," Nathan said appreciatively. Dr. Vegatillius still had not let go of his hand, which was now shaking like the head of an epileptic woodpecker. "I have come to see you about my mind. I would like you to certify that I am not insane."

"Well, I'm not a miracle worker but I'll have a crack at it anyway." Finally the doctor let go of Nathan's hand, which had turned an unnatural shade of maroon.

"And what about you?" he asked, turning to Brian. "Are you insane?"

"No."

"Would you like to be?"

"No."

"Well, if you change your mind let me know and I can change your mind."

Vegatillius led them into a room with a man swearing at a

parrot.

"This is our language sciences lab," Vegatillius explained as he led them swiftly past. "We have to share the space with them. Most other animal studies are upstairs. Graduate housing is the floor above that. Nuisance but there you have it."

He guided them through a second room filled with microscopes, petri dishes, chemicals, and up a flight of stairs. This room was very spacious and open. It seemed they were back on the ground floor. Light was streaming in through the windows. It had several large and sophisticated medical-looking machines, with huge shiny white parts and smooth contours and computers and such. Dr. Vegatillius ignored all of these and sat Nathan down in a grubby chair with a desk in front of it. He put three items on the desk. They looked to be a colander, a flashlight, and a hammer.

"What's that?" Brian asked, pointing at the colander.

"That's an EEG cap. The inside is coated with a variety of high sensitivity electrodes that will allow me to map neural activity and transmit it to the computer system."

"Oh. And what's that?" He indicated the flashlight.

"That is an extremely powerful and experimental tool called a handheld diffuse optical imaging - or DOI - scanner. It uses the scattering of infrared light and biophotonics to scan the patient's brain when I press it against his head."

"And what's that?"

"That's a hammer, in case the patient gets any funny ideas."

Dr. Vegatillius then measured Nathan's brain with the EEG cap and the DOI scanner while periodically threatening him with the hammer. While this was a hideously technically complicated and sophisticated process, it appeared to the two laymen that Dr. Vegatillius just ran the scanner all over Nathan, then plopped the EEG cap down on his head, all the while making a very loud and obnoxious buzzing noise with his teeth and lips.

The buzzing noise was absolutely necessary for a myriad of reasons that there isn't enough time to go into right now.

When he'd finished making the buzzing noise and pulled off the EEG cap, Dr. Vegatillius began to explain.

"Now, you asked me to certify that you are not insane. I cannot, strictly speaking, do that. I can take pictures of your brain and certify that your brain lesion will not - by itself - cause you to be insane, but that doesn't mean you're not insane. You still could have gone insane normally, like the rest of us."

"Really?" Nathan asked. "Darn it. I was really hoping that you could demonstrate I wasn't insane. I have to avoid filling out some paperwork, you see."

"And I sympathize entirely - half of what I do must be avoiding paperwork - but what you really want is a psychologist."

This, coincidentally, marked the only time in the history of human civilization that a neurobiologist has ever said, "what you really want is a psychologist," but the occasion went mostly unnoticed by all but a few media outlets.

"So you can't certify me as not insane?"

"No. You need a psychologist. Unfortunately, my doctorate is in art history, and I can't help you. Ah, and I've got some lovely pictures of your lesion," Dr. Vegatillius said, showing them on a nearby screen. It was blank.

"There's nothing there," Brian complained.

"Yes. That is what makes it a lesion." He paused. "I'd like to get a few functional images of your brain. Would you just sit down in the PET scanner? There we go. Nice and slowly. Don't make me use the hammer."

Nathan sat down in the PET scanner, an apparatus which dwarfed his head.

"This is a positron emission tomography scanner. Now put out your arm. I'm going to inject you with a fast-acting radiotracer."

The doctor pressed his needle into Nathan's arm and a dark dye shot into Nathan's bloodstream.

"That was a contrast dye," Dr. Vegatillius explained. "It is a radioisotope that emits a form of antimatter called a positron. When these positrons collide with nearby electrons, they annihilate each other with an amount of energy that is greater per unit mass than a nuclear warhead. Then I pick up the little explosions on my radiation scanner."

"Really?" Nathan asked.

"Yes, really?"

"Really really?"

"Really."

This is not really how positron emission tomography works. In real PET, the radiotracer is administered further in advance and, generally speaking, by a man who knows what he's doing.

Nathan sat and waited while Dr. Vegatillius manned a nearby computer console and tapped furiously at his keyboard. He started humming again, for the same important reasons as last time. After a few minutes, the computer made a loud dinging noise, which Nathan took to mean that the scan was done.

"Incredible," Dr. Vegatillius exclaimed.

"What is?" Brian asked.

"This is a very healthy, normal PET scan. Very healthy indeed." He pressed a button. "But enough about that. I'd better take a look at yours instead, Nathan..."

He peered at it. Like all doctors, he now had good news and bad news.

"Well, the good news is that I can definitely declare that your brain damage is not sufficient cause to declare you insane. Here, let me write you a note to that effect." He very quickly scrawled out a note certifying that Nathan was not insane due to brain damage.

"What's the bad news?" Nathan asked as he took the note.

Dr. Vegatillius did not immediately answer.

Thanks to his access to the PET scan, Dr. Vegatillius saw part of the very disastrous thing that was about to happen shortly before it happened. It turned out that the highly radioactive fludeoxyglucose tracer that had been used as contrast dye in the PET scan had accidentally been mixed with Baker's Choice brand corn starch due to manufacturing error, and subsequently thickened. As a result of this thickening, Nathan was about to have a stroke and Dr. Vegatillius was about to regret that, unlike the bureaucrats of the next world, he had not had the foresight or wisdom to try to get Nathan to sign a liability waiver. Then again, the people of the city really didn't put up with that sort of thing, and the motto of Dead Donkey's medical researchers had long been, "shoot 'em all and let God sort 'em out."

Nathan's head lolled to one side as his stroke began.

"What is he doing?" Brian asked sharply.

Dr. Vegatillius consulted the PET scan.

"Dying," he reported shortly.

It was at this point that a confluence of other factors that

Nathan was previously aware of but did not regard as important - namely that they were adjacent to the ground floor animal testing laboratories and below the second floor graduate residences - and factors that Nathan was not aware of - namely that the ground floor animal cages were made by the same people who'd "made" the animal cages for Dead Donkey's zoo, and that the ceiling had not been built to code - resulted in Nathan's demise.

Nathan was rapidly losing consciousness principally due to the fact that he was having a stroke, although he was also feeling quite tired after all this walking around and such. The last thing he heard before he fell into darkness was Brian's voice as he suddenly looked up towards the nearby open window.

"Is that a badger?"

A badger had just come through the window and, as it happened, was rather angry and slightly embarrassed about the hairstyling experiment that several sociologists had been conducting on it and decided to take out its frustrations on the nearest person to itself. The badger started to maul Nathan's face.

At exactly the same time, one of the faulty bathtubs that had been made by Nathan's second grandfather came crashing through the ceiling above him. Its fault was that it did not drain properly, but instead leaked onto the floor above them, weakening the ceiling - which as mentioned had not been built to code - until the ceiling gave way. It then managed to completely miss both Brian and Dr. Vegatillius but hit Nathan squarely, crushing him and the badger.

And so Nathan died.

Chapter 14

Though the bureaucrats of the afterlife run reality - making sure all the right atoms smash into all the other right atoms and so on - they have very little actual leeway. Generally speaking, they HAVE to make such and such an atom smash into such and such another atom at just such an angle to be in compliance with the universal laws that they exist to uphold, and cannot actually influence events even though they have the power to make them happen. Therefore, there is very little point in blaming them when something bad happens, like when you catch the flu or when your house falls on your dog. These things are simply the effects of the logical causes that created them: shaking hands with a hobo and hoisting your house above your dog, respectively.

However, the bureaucrats do actually have tremendous discretionary power in one and only one aspect of life: sports. The universal laws say nothing about sports, which generally but not always consist of the transfer of balls from one location to another. There is no particular mandate for how these events need to play out, and so the bureaucrats have vast power in the filing of the form 288026: Instrument Determining the Result of a Sporting Match. This means that during a sport, absolutely anything can happen. The ball may explode. The referees may discover a new and previously unmentioned rule that allows players to use jetpacks. One player can fall in love with, and marry, another. Coaches may be allowed to switch teams without notice. Cricket - an activity that literally no human would ever think to engage in if it were anything but a sport - draws the attention of millions worldwide. Etc. etc. etc. While this is one of the reasons that sports are so exciting, and so many of the classic sporting moments in history have been so truly bizarre and unexpected, it also means that literally every sporting match that has ever been played has been rigged (or, counting the influence of the gamblers, rigged twice).

Unfortunately, this also means that all of the pre-game: the assemblage of players and practice and the determination of the team, amounts of steroids taken, etc., is more or less irrelevant unless it impresses the bureaucrats. A team of girl scouts stands on equal footing with an NBA all-star team if it pleases and amuses the bureaucrats. Fortunately, the bureaucrats are often impressed by hard work and displays of physical athleticism and sometimes decide the game on merits. More often they just pick whoever amuses them, or whoever has filed their tax returns properly that year.

The other exciting implication of this revelation is that virtually anything can be changed by rendering it a sport. If the economy were declared a sport, anything would be possible: the Americans and the Chinese would be favored for the win this year, but they might be upset by the Tuvaluans at the last moment in a startling come-from-behind victory that future generations of economics fans would enjoy.

Nathan had always hated sports, which is why his life was so drearily predictable, though the significance of this was lost on him as he made his way to the afterlife once again.

Chapter 15

"Station negative two please," the loudspeaker voice rang out. Nathan materialized in front of a desk with a severe-looking gray-haired middle-aged woman in a mauve blouse behind it. A sign identified it as the Desk for People Who Died of Badger Attack While Simultaneously Having A Stroke And A Bathtub Fall On Their Heads.

Jeanne (the woman in the mauve blouse) barely looked up as she thrust a form at him.

"Name, type of badger, type of stroke, type of bathtub," she said, ticking off the boxes he needed to fill out with her pen.

Sadly, Nathan was not paying much attention to her. He was still being mauled by the badger. His response therefore went something like, "Auuughhh, why are its claws so sharp?"

Despite the hideous pain, it did briefly cross Nathan's mind to wonder exactly why the badger had come with him to the bureaucratic death offices when the bathtub had not and, similarly, he was no longer having a stroke.

The Vatican has long answered the sorrowful questions of young children grieving at the loss of a pet cat or dog by cruelly insisting that only ensouled creatures go to heaven, that these animals do not have souls, and that they are therefore banished to the void when they die. While they are absolutely correct (provided that the necessary Form 12234 - Banishment Of Beloved Pet To Void is filled out in triplicate), it turns out that humans are not the only ensouled creature. Badgers also have souls. Dogs, cats, gerbils, budgies, etc., do not. It is only humans and badgers. Badgers are therefore entitled to consultation with and technical assistance from the afterworld bureaucrats, in much the same way as humans are. This mandate has caused some difficulty for the bureaucrats, because while they might have souls, badgers are not particularly fond of tedious paperwork, and getting them to sign forms is almost as difficult as getting Nathan to sign. Fortunately, their signatures can usually be bartered for a stoat, which keeps the wheels of cosmic bureaucracy turning at their usual efficient pace.

This was also the reason that even though Nathan had died, the badger was still mauling him. As strokes and bathtubs only very rarely have souls, they obviously did not come with him.

"And then I need your signature on the bottom," Jeanne explained as Nathan rolled around in agony.

"Auughhh!" he replied. "Why does it have claws on its feet too?"

"You're lucky," the man from one desk down (the ebola desk), said as he watched Nathan roll around. "I haven't gotten a single one all week."

Jeanne appeared unimpressed with Nathan's tortured screaming.

"Very well," she said. Her tone was businesslike but tinged with repressed loathing, much like the frumpy woman at station four's had been. "I can see you will need some assistance filling out this form." She peered over at the badger which was at present still biting hard into his neck. "Type of badger - North American *taxidea taxus*. Type of person - approximately thirty year old caucasian male. And if I recall correctly your name is Nathan Haynes. Do I have that right?"

"Yes," Nathan gasped.

"Good. What was the type of bathtub?"

"Porcelain enamel and cast iron wall fixture," he managed to yell between screams. With great effort, he wrenched the badger off his chest, though it continued to strike at his arms like - well, an angry badger. Due to the fact that he was dead, the badger attack had left no wounds on his person, and because of his brain damage, he almost immediately forgot about it.

"And type of stroke?" she asked.

"I don't know. My doctor just said it was a stroke."

"Unspecified," she muttered. "Oh dear, well, I'll have to ask a few more questions."

Because Nathan had forgotten how painful it was to be attacked by the badger, he let down his guard and the badger slipped out of his hands. It landed on his chest and started to maul him again.

"May I ask your marital status?" she said.

"I'm single," Nathan said.

Jeanne adjusted her glasses in agitation.

"I was speaking to the badger."

The badger growled.

"Unmarried. I see. Do you have any children?"

It growled again.

"Two adopted."

It growled a third time.

The bureaucrat adjusted her glasses.

"I do not," she said crossly, "need to hear your life story."

She checked off several more boxes and then handed the form to the badger. Things went on in this vein for about half an hour, with her asking the badger various questions about its dependents, family, immigration status, insurance, and so on until she had finally finished.

"You are dead," she told it. "Sign here please."

It scratched through the signature box with one of its foot

claws and disappeared. Nathan was very grateful for this, because when the badger vanished it stopped mauling him. He stood up and dusted himself off a bit.

"Where did it go?"

"To badger receiving," replied Jeanne.

"Er... how is that different from here?"

The clerk adjusted her glasses.

"Obviously it is staffed by badgers. It only came to human receiving because you both died together."

"Oh. Right."

"Now back to your form. You are dead. Sign here please."

She pushed a form towards Nathan. It said "Form 21AYC - Acknowledgment and Waiver Of Liability Subsequent To Dying of Concurrent Stroke, Falling Bathtub, and Badger Attack (for human)"

There was a time when Nathan would have regarded this form as silly, but now that he had actually died of CSTFBABA he felt quite grateful that they had been thoughtful enough to set up a special desk and paperwork for it. Still, he wasn't feeling grateful enough to actually sign the form liked he was supposed to.

"I'm not signing anything," he said stubbornly.

"You have to sign it," she insisted.

"But I won't. I've already been through all this before. That's why I came to see you a few hours ago. Why don't you just send me to Director Fulcher? Then I can get this all sorted out."

"Protocol must be followed," Jeanne said menacingly. She thrust the form at him very insistently.

"He's telling the truth, Jeanne," said the man from the desk on the right side. Nathan recalled that this was the desk for affairs pertaining to Mr. Travis Erwin Habsworth, of 2388 Shillington Road, Albany. Its attendant seemed to have taken his view of things.

"Stay out of this, Warren," she spat at him.

"Director Fulcher said if this Nathan fellow showed up again he should be directed straight to his office. It was in this memorandum."

Warren rummaged around his desk, knocking aside documents labelled "Notice You Are About To Receive A Memorandum," "Notice You Are About to Receive A Notice That You Are About to Receive A Memorandum," and "Verification That You Have Received A Memorandum." He eventually found a document that was simply labelled "Memorandum: Nathan Haynes of Dead Donkey, Nevada." Warren slapped it with his knuckles.

"It says that if Nathan Haynes of Dead Donkey, Nevada arrives at any receiving desk and refuses to sign his form, he should be sent to the director's office immediately."

Jeanne sniffed airily.

"I did not receive the Response To the Verification Of Receipt of Memorandum," she said.

"Oh for god sake's, Jeanne," Warren said testily. "There's more to life than paperwork."

The room (which had several other bureaucrats' desks in it) suddenly went deadly silent. Everyone glared at Warren as if he'd said something dirty.

"You would say that, wouldn't you, Warren?" she spat. "That's why they put you at the Travis Erwin Habsworth desk."

"Who is-" Nathan started, but Jeanne turned her evil eye back on him.

"Fine," she said. "I will send you to Director Fulcher's

office. But if you are ever simultaneously crushed by a bathtub, mauled by a badger, and killed by a stroke again don't come crying to me!"

Nathan blinked and in the next moment he was standing outside of Director Fulcher's office.

Chapter 16

Director Fulcher regarded Nathan severely from over the polished top of his frightfully clean desk.

"I am beginning to think that you are suffering from a point of confusion, Mr. Haynes. You may be interested to know that the average life expectancy for someone living in your country is more than seventy years. You have died three times in one afternoon."

"It's all been very interesting," Nathan said brightly. "I got to meet a badger."

"Yes, well, unfortunately for you, our little game is nearly at its end."

"Are we playing Monopoly again?"

Fulcher held his head in his hands.

"There is no Monopoly involved," he said. "No Monopoly."

"Operation then? Do you have one of those gameboards with the little buzzers?"

The director took several very deep breaths.

"The point is this. We have nearly filed the forms necessary to declare you insane in the mandated dodecduplicate, at which point I will have power of attorney over you and be able to sign your 21B on your behalf. Then this will all be over."

"Oh no, I don't think so." Nathan smiled genially. "I have this note from my doctor that says I'm not insane."

He reached into his pocket and found that although he had died the note was still there. He handed it to Fulcher.

Fulcher read it with a deepening frown.

"You were examined?"

"Yes. He took a PET and an EEG and told me I was A-

OKAY."

"Who is this man Dr. Vegatillius?"

"He is my doctor."

"Is he a medical doctor?"

"He's an art historian."

"Blast." Director Fulcher stared at it furiously. "But this isn't adequate," he announced at last. "It doesn't say that you aren't insane, just that your brain damage doesn't render you insane. You might still be insane in one of the usual ways. That, Mr. Haynes, is what we in the business call a loophole." He grinned evilly.

Nathan was nodding.

"Oh yes, I already know about that. But the last time I was here, you said you'd read my file and found out about my brain damage, and decided that was the reason I was insane. So I suppose you have prepared all of your paperwork assuming that is the cause of my alleged insanity."

The smile vanished from Fulcher's face. He suddenly looked very grim.

"Touche, Mr. Haynes. My hat is off to you." A large tophat materialized on his head, which he briefly took off before it disappeared again. "However, the evidence speaks for itself. You must be insane. What other possible explanation can there be for your repeated deaths? Your reckless disregard for danger? Your stubborn intransigence? Your awful dress sense?"

Nathan looked down at his clothes. He thought they looked fine.

"You have bought yourself a few hours at the most," the director continued.

"Oh, but you can't have me here for a few hours," Nathan replied. He felt he was catching on to this whole bureaucracy thing. "I might sue you. I've already been attacked by a badger on your premises."

Fulcher sat up very stiffly. "I think you will find that is wholly the fault of the badger in question, and this department is not at all liable for any injury you might have suffered, physical or otherwise."

"Oh, but Mr. Fulcher, I was only attacked because I was left waiting in line behind the badger. I understand you circulated a memorandum to have me brought directly to your office if I arrived here again, but Ms. Jeanne failed to do so because of a communication error. I was subsequently attacked by the badger. If your staff had properly executed their duties I would have been fine. Isn't that negligence on the part of your department?"

"Damn your eyes," Fulcher swore.

Nathan smiled. He felt very clever for once. Indeed, this was all very good reasoning for a man who had just had a stroke.

Fulcher whipped out a form and filled it out furiously.

"We will settle the matter of the badger later," he said angrily. "In the mean time I am sending you back."

"Good. When I get back I will find a psychologist to declare me sane and healthy."

The director snorted. "No psychologist in the world would declare you sane. The whole field of psychology is built on the concept of finding things wrong with people."

With that he signed the form and the world started to fade around Nathan. But Nathan, who felt like he was on something of a roll, decided he wanted the last word.

"You have never met a Dead Donkey psychologist," he called into the void.

And then he was back.

Chapter 17

Physics holds that the faster you go, the slower time goes, and that if you go close to the speed of light time goes very slowly, and that you cannot go faster than the speed of light but if you ever do you go back in time.

This idea was first introduced by Albert Einstein a very high speed ago. He was able to demonstrate that it was true through empirical observation, but his explanations for why exactly it worked the way he said it did tended to involve analogies with people bouncing balls in elevators or staring at moving trains, and were therefore very confusing and/or dangerous.

While it is pointedly true that time moves slower the faster you go (as any person who has ever been on a jetliner cross-continent can attest), it is not for the reasons Einstein said it was. The real reason time moves slower the faster you go has nothing to do with either balls bouncing in elevators or staring at moving trains and is instead a product of bureaucracy. If you are simply moving, then the cosmic bureaucrats only have to fill out a few hundred easy forms about why you are going to Atlantic City, why you are going in a 1990s Chevy, why you have a corked baseball bat in the trunk, etc, and things run fairly smoothly. However, if you go very fast (say, close to the speed of light), things become much more complicated, because the bureaucrats have to fill out the forms faster, and explain not only why you are going to Atlantic City but also to Reno, New Orleans, Atlantic City again, and ultimately Blackpool in the UK, which has a whole and spectacular new set of forms associated with it. The fact of the matter is that the bureaucrats can only fill in so many forms so quickly, so they generally agree to slow time to give themselves time to process the paperwork. While it still looks like you are going very fast to everyone you left behind when you converted the 1990s Chevy to a near-lightspeed-capable supercraft, you are moving very fast so they can't see you very well, and the bureaucrats have in fact sped up everything else so they don't get suspicious and it all averages out to normal.

It was exactly this sort of trick that Director Fulcher now proposed to play on Nathan. Nathan's reply had spooked him, and he was afraid that Nathan would in fact be able to find some complete quack of a psychologist to certify him as sane, therefore ruining all of Director Fulcher's careful efforts and shaming his department. However, the paperwork to slow down time is so immensely complicated and involves so many circuitous forms (such as Form 99493 - Authorization To Temporarily Distract All Physicists and Form 62344 - Instrument To Hide Luminous Ether) that Director Fulcher realized that it would be both faster and easier to simply fill out the forms to declare Nathan insane.

However, he was still worried about the psychologist, so he decided to play an entirely different sort of trick on Nathan.

Chapter 18

Nathan popped back into existence exactly where he had died, quite near the bathtub manufactured by his second grandfather that had recently crushed himself and a mostly innocent if very angry badger. Happily, the badger had not been returned to life with him.

"Hello," he said.

"Oh, er, you're back," Dr. Vegatillius stuttered. He hurriedly hid the insidious instrument he had been about to use to probe dead Nathan's brain behind his back. "Brian told me that you might be, but I didn't really believe him."

"What were you doing with that little wire?"

"Um - nothing. Nothing at all. I mean, I enjoy holding little wires near corpses. It's my hobby. Coincidentally, do you think you will be needing your old body?"

"No," Nathan said.

"Splendid," Vegatillius said brightly, and turned back to the body to do some other things that would appear horrific to less scientific minds. He started to make the loud humming noise again.

"Do you have a psychology department around here?" Nathan asked.

"Oh yes, just down the hall. Past the karekliology lab."

"The what?"

"The karekliology lab." Vegatillius gestured energetically.

Just as there are fields of study in science that the public assumes to be real but are in fact bunk, there are areas of science that the public knows nothing about but are highly legitimate areas of research. Karekliology is the study of chairs. It is one of the most aggressive, profitable, and it must be said comfortable areas of science, and has propelled our understanding of chairs forward enormously in the past few years. Karekliology seeks to answer the big questions about chairs - why do they exist? Who made them? Where are they going?

Members of the general public tend to derisively answer these questions, "to sit on," "Ikea," and "nowhere," respectively, which is why karekliologists keep to themselves. If your son or daughter ever says they have decided to pursue a liberal sciences degree (which they will endeavor to convince you is the science equivalent of a liberal arts degree), note that this is code. They have entered the noble field of karekliology, and are probably doing splendid work on any number of top secret government karekliology projects, like developing a new and even lazier Boy Recliner, or a comfy chair that can be lounged in in zero-gravity so America's astronauts are well equipped for space leisure. Do not question or disrupt their efforts. It is vitally important that they be allowed to finish their work as quickly as possible to maintain our country's lead over the communists.

Dr. Vegatillius showed Nathan where the karekliology lab was. Outside, Brian was watching a man being swung around a giant spinning machine in an armchair.

"You understand that it is very important that the chairs be tested under the most extreme conditions," Vegatillius said. "All very hush-hush. Let's not linger."

He hurried them on.

Near the end of the hallway they reached a sign that indicated they had reached the Dead Donkey Milton Prodmany Center Psychology Division. Due to an extreme shortage of space, the psychologists had been placed in the same building as the neurologists, even though neither group could bear the other. Border friction had culminated in the great First Floor War of '08, in which the neurologists had attempted to annex the psychologists into neurology but had eventually been convinced to withdraw after the psychologists started asking them about their mothers. Thereafter the janitorial department had been sent in as peacekeepers. Two janitors were in fact standing guard in front of the Psychology Division now. They crossed their brooms to prevent Dr. Vegatillius from entering.

"I'm afraid this is as far as I go," he called out, "I'll just go back to the lab and probe- er, I mean, properly bury your body."

"Good idea," Nathan said. Dr. Vegatillius withdrew rapidly. Nathan and Brian were left to enter the psychology department alone. There was no waiting room or laboratory area in the psychology department that Nathan could see. Instead, all there was in the front room was one of those long couches with the inclined heads that psychologists always seem to have. (This flies in the face of the advice of karekliologists, who insist they should use a different model for optimal effect, but the psychologists have a bulk discount at this point and aren't willing to get new ones.)

No sooner had Nathan and Brian entered the room than a man with a little beard and psychologists' spectacles emerged from the corner, where he had apparently been hiding.

"Tell me about your parents," he demanded of Brian.

Brian stood very still.

"I hate my parents," he said stiffly.

"Indeed! Well, we must admit you at once. Come, come."

And the bearded man steered Brian into a back room at great speed.

Nathan was now left alone in the psychologist's office. The cereal jingle he had been hearing earlier started to play in his head, though it was now accompanied by Dr. Vegatillius' buzzing noise for some reason.

After a few minutes, a dark-haired woman in a heavy suit entered the room. She, like the psychologist from before, was wearing a pair of little glasses and a little false beard.

"Tell me about your mother," she demanded of Nathan immediately.

"I never knew my mother," Nathan said.

"Goodness, we must admit you at once."

"I was hoping that you could certify me as not insane," Nathan continued.

"Of course, of course," she replied. "Just pop into this straightjacket for me."

She held up a straightjacket covered with buckles and things.

Nathan thought about this for a while.

"You know, I think I'd rather not," he said, after due consideration.

The psychologist whipped out a notepad.

"Displays... irrational... aversion... to... authority," she wrote on the notepad.

"I don't think that's quite fair," Nathan said.

"Questions... the... judgement... of... experts," she continued.

"Anyway," Nathan pushed on, "I must have a piece of paper saying that I'm not insane or otherwise the bureaucrats who run reality will declare me insane and the next time I die they won't have to ask for me to sign my 21B - they'll be able to sign it for me! I've died three times today already, you see."

"Oh yes, of course," the woman nodded, without writing anything. "Well, we'll get you fixed up in no time. Come with me."

She led him into a room that was in every respect identical to the one they had just left, except that there was a watercolor picture of an almond on the wall of the new room, and there had not been in the old one.

"Why is there a picture of an almond in this room?" Nathan asked as the woman directed him onto the couch.

"Because this is the room for nuts," the woman said calmly.

Nathan felt insulted and indignant, but on the other hand it was a very good picture of an almond, so he didn't get too worked up about it. In fact, it made him feel a little hungry.

"My name is Dr. April. Please tell me what you see." She held up a white canvas with a large black ink blot.

"It's a large black ink blot," Nathan said.

"Correct!" Dr. April said brightly. "You'd be surprised how many people don't get that right."

"Am I sane then?"

"Not quite yet I'm afraid," she said apologetically. "We've only just started. Let's do some simple word association. I say a word and then you say the first word that springs to mind. Here's the first one. Banana."

"Banana," Nathan said immediately.

"White."

"White!" he replied enthusiastically.

"Star."

"Star." Nathan started to smile. He felt he was rather good at this.

"Very interesting," Dr. April scribbled down on her notepad. "Now, when did you first start to worry that you might be insane?"

"When Director Fulcher said that if I were insane that he would be able to sign a form without my consent."

"And why did he think you might be insane?"

"He found out about my brain damage. I have a lesion, you see. You must ask Dr. Vegatillius about it. He has the results of my PET scan. I had a stroke, got mauled by a badger, then was crushed by a bathtub during the scan though. Still, it must be worth a look."

A rather pained expression crossed Dr. April's face.

"I'm afraid I can't."

"Why not?"

"Cooperation between the neurology and psychology departments hasn't been very good recently."

"Oh. I'm sorry to hear about it."

"Don't worry about it. It will all be over soon. In fact, it's only a matter of time before we expel the janitors from the buffer zone and then march upon the neurobiologists and take revenge for the humiliation they inflicted on us during the War, and the corridors will run atrocious crimson and stink of their fetid blood."

"Well, good luck with that," Nathan said brightly.

"Thank you," Dr. April said equally brightly, adjusting her fake beard as she spoke. "Now, are you married or unmarried?"

"Unmarried."

"I noticed you came in here with another rather attractive young man. Do you think you could be compelled to seek out male company because of your latent homosexuality?"

"Oh no, I don't think so," Nathan answered conversationally. "I wish Brian would go away, you see. He's following me without my consent. He was sent by the bureaucrats to monitor me."

"Are you sure? Have you kept the company of any other unmarried young men recently?"

"I was mauled to death by an unmarried badger," Nathan recalled.

Dr. April scrawled something down on her notepad.

"Were you made to feel guilty about things as a child?"

"Oh no, not at all. In fact, I hardly did anything out of the ordinary. My father used to worry that I wasn't committing arsons like the other boys."

There was more scrawling.

"And how would you describe your relationship with your father?"

"I think he and I got along very well until he died choking on that candy."

"Did that make you feel angry? Scared?"

"I was very sad. I wasn't angry, and as I was trying to say earlier, because of my condition I don't feel fear of death. I suppose that normal people must be very scared of candy. I guess they must just think to themselves, 'why I could choke on a tiny piece of candy any time and that would be the end of me.'"

"But you aren't scared of candy?"

"I'm not scared of death at all because of my lesion. Also, I've died three times now and it wasn't so bad. There was a lot of paperwork involved, though."

"So you're not scared of death?"

"No."

"Do you think about killing yourself?"

"No, not at all. I don't really like Director Fulcher so I don't want to see him very often. Besides, I've already seen him three times today. Why do you ask? Do you think about killing yourself sometimes?"

Dr. April paused in her scribblings.

"Oh, all the time but only so I can be with my husband and brother and beloved pet dog Rover.'

"I'm sorry. Did they die?"

"Oh no. They're all at home. I just work long hours. But let's talk about you, not me."

"If you like," Nathan said pleasantly. "I do wish we could hurry it up a bit though. I suppose Director Fulcher could finish having me declared insane at any moment."

"Don't worry. We're almost done. Do you hear voices?"

"Lots of voices."

"Whose voices do you hear?"

"Yours, for example."

"I see. And do you ever feel that other people are watching you?"

"I suspect that lots of people are watching me all the time," Nathan said.

"And why is that?"

"I don't know, but they somehow manage to not bump into me when I walk through crowds of them, so I think they must be looking at me."

"And do you feel safe in your own home?"

"Oh yes. Mr. Fletcher kills nearly everyone who comes onto the street who might be dangerous, although a serial killer did break into my home twice today. He was such a nice serial killer though. I hardly think we can count him."

"Do you think people are out to get you?"

"I know they are. I've spoken to them."

"Have you been sleeping well recently?"

"Yes, except that Mr. Fletcher keeps waking me up. He has a shotgun, you see."

"Are you sick? Do you feel well?"

"I just had a stroke a few minutes ago. Is that what you're talking about?"

"No, no, just a routine question. Coincidentally, who is your healthcare provider?"

"I'm afraid I live on a disability pension related to my brain damage."

"Oh dear, well then that's about all we have time for," Dr. April said, quickly closing up her notebook. "I'll have to ask you to agree to let me publish an article about all of this to make it worth my while."

"Am I insane?" Nathan asked.

"You have an Oedipus complex and Asperger's syndrome; you are a latent homosexual, a paranoid schizophrenic, violently psychotic, and a hypochondriac. But other than that, yes, I'm happy to say you are completely sane."

"Hooray," Nathan said happily. "Could you give me something to show to Mr. Fulcher so he can't declare me insane?"

"Yes, of course, I'll have it prepared straight away. Just go out and wait in the lobby and I'll send my nurse to bring it to you."

"What about all those other things you said I had?"

"Oh, there's a cream for those," Dr. April reassured him. "I'll have him bring that out too."

Nathan went back out and waited in the lobby (which looked exactly the same except it did not have the picture of an almond). The first person to come out and join him was not a nurse but Brian. He looked extremely unhappy.

"What's wrong?" Nathan asked him.

"They told me I have obsessive compulsive disorder," he said with a huff. "As if." He straightened his tie. "What about you?"

"Oh, they told me I'm sane," Nathan said.

Brian's eyebrows disappeared into his hair.

"If you're sane, what do insane people look like?" he asked.

Nathan was about to reply when a form materialized in his hands. He stared at it, then handed it to Brian.

"It's for you. It says you're about to receive a notice regarding a memorandum."

Brian looked and frowned at it. "Why would they go to all the trouble to send me one of these?" he asked.

No sooner had he spoken the words than another form appeared in his hands.

"It's a notice that I'm about to receive a memorandum," he said, his frown deepening.

A third form appeared in his hands.

"What does it say," Nathan asked, craning his head to look at it.

"It says I'm about to get a phone call," Brian said.

His pocket began to ring with a slow, functional tune. He fished out an old-looking flip phone.

"Hello?" he said. There was a pause. "Here? But why? How?"

He was now looking very upset and somewhat afraid. He wandered out of the room still speaking into the phone, his hand groping at the little satchel he wore that contained a large stack of forms.

Nathan watched him go with interest, then went back to

waiting.

After a few minutes, a dark-haired male nurse emerged from a side door. From just outside the room, Brian - though he was still on the phone - turned and frowned at the nurse.

"Here you go," the nurse said. "Here is the paperwork declaring you sane, and here is your cream. I should explain that this is a topical cream. Apply directly to your brain to get best results."

"Thank you," Nathan said, pocketing the cream.

The nurse held out a clipboard.

"Let me explain that this is the paperwork declaring you to be sane," the nurse said and flipped through several pages to the last page. "Dr. April has already signed, but I'm afraid you need to sign right there."

He handed Nathan a pen. Nathan signed.

As he did this, he simultaneously became aware of several things he hadn't previously noticed. First, Brian was frowning at the male nurse with a look of recognition in his eyes. Second, the male nurse had a familiar aura of authority and hopelessness about him. And third, he was wearing a tie - a tie done up with the immensely complicated triple Windsor knot.

"You!" Nathan gasped, springing up. "You're Ian!"

Ian was momentarily taken aback, but snatched up the form and grinned broadly. "Yes, Mr. Haynes. Very good. You recognized me. This was a deception. Let me explain that a deception is a trick-"

"I know what a deception is. What are you doing here?"

"Ah. I should explain that I was given a temporary body to enter this world for the purpose of deceiving you into thinking I was a nurse and getting you to sign paperwork that you thought would declare you sane, but was actually a 21B. It was

Director Fulcher's plan. I feel I should explain that a plan-"

"I know what a plan is! That was a dirty trick."

"It was," Ian agreed. "But it doesn't matter now that you've signed the form! Your 21B is all signed and filled out," he said, patting it appreciatively. "This is the end for you, Mr. Haynes. Now the next time you die your paperwork will be in order."

"Noooooo," Nathan said. "Not that! Anything but that."

"I'm afraid so, Mr. Haynes. We have won this round. I should explain winning is the attainment of victory, which is what we have done! You should have known better than to go up against the forces of bureaucracy."

No sooner had he said this than the side door opened. Through it walked a middle aged man who Nathan had never seen before. He had dark, somewhat graying hair, and he was tall, very tall, thin and fit. His eyes were determined and powerful, and he had a kind of quiet presence that filled the room. He was not wearing a tie. With unflappable deliberation he walked up to Ian. Ian did not notice him.

"Now that I have this form my mission here is complete," Ian continued. "I should explain complete means finished, terminated satisfactorily. Your 21B will be filed and-"

The newcomer grabbed the form from Ian's hands and neatly tore it into tiny shreds.

Ian whipped around.

"You can't just do that!" he said to the newcomer, aghast. "Who do you think you are?"

The new man looked him straight in the eyes.

"I am Mr. Travis Erwin Habsworth, of 2388 Shillington Road, Albany."

Chapter 19

Mr. Travis Erwin Habsworth of 2388 Shillington Road, Albany, is one of the most singularly extraordinary people to walk the earth, because of one completely unique quality that he possesses. His parents died when he was little, and he was subsequently brought up in foster care. During that upbringing, due to an accident involving an arson, a sociologist, and a copy of Adam Smith's *The Wealth of Nations,* he does not believe in money.

There are many people who say that they do not believe in money, by which they usually mean that they think humanity either should use gold as money because gold is very shiny and therefore valuable or else mean humanity shouldn't use any sort of money at all and should instead work for some utopian notion of a common good. (Funnily, these tend to be the exact opposite sorts of people in all other respects.) This is not what Mr. Habsworth believes. Unlike these other people who say they do not believe in money but actually simply disagree with it, Mr. Habsworth actually does not believe in money. That is, he does not believe money exists. He does not think that people in fact and on a day to day basis exchange pieces of paper with pictures of dead Presidents on them in return for goods and services. He thinks that people do all the things they do - grow food and cut hedges and build smartphones and whatnot for some as-yet-unidentified and inscrutable reason that has nothing whatsoever to do with pictures of dead Presidents. In his opinion, to the extent that people have to settle debts between themselves, they do so with little pieces of string and pictures of cats on the internet. He decided that this is the only rational reason that there could possibly be so many pictures of cats on the internet. While he is right that this is the only *rational* reason that there could be so many pictures of cats on the internet, it is not the actual reason that there are so many pictures of cats on the internet, making Mr. Habsworth both right and wrong at the same time. This is something of a trend with him.

Mr. Habsworth is of course wrong that money does not exist. In fact, owing to his belief that money does not exist, Mr. Habsworth is the second wrongest man alive. The wrongest man alive is Professor Stephen Hawking, formerly Lucasian Professor of Mathematics and now researcher of the Center For Theoretical Cosmology at the University of Cambridge, periodic contributing lecturer at the California Institute of Technology, etc. He believes that within the universe there are peculiar gravitationally bound singularities called black holes, formed by the collapse of massive bodies, which store and can release information. Professor Hawking believes this so strongly that he has staked money on it (something that Mr. Habsworth refuses to believe he has done). In fact, black holes are not caused by any sort of collapse except for a collapse in the bureaucratic filing system. In short, black holes are where the cosmic bureaucrats who manage reality hide their completed and historical forms. Since they have a quizillion of these, they quickly ran out of space in their storage rooms and needed to invent a new kind of storage system that would allow them to put a substantial fraction of a quizillion forms into an infinitely small area. So they invented black holes, and to make sure that no one would ever be able to remove forms from the storage areas without the proper authorization forms filled out in triplicate, they made them impossible to leave. Since the forms to remove other forms from black holes are extremely complicated and involve such circuitous relationships as "Form 973970 - Form to Receive a Form 885134," and "Form 885134 - Form to Receive a Form 973970," and "Form 617525 - Destroy At Least Two Other Form 617525s To Receive This Form," it is exceedingly unlikely anyone will ever be able to retrieve information from them. If Prof. Hawking had known this, he would probably have given up on the field of cosmology entirely and started playing badminton. In many ways it's a pity he didn't, because he would have won what would have generally been regarded as the greatest upset victory in the history of Olympic badminton and finally furnished the world with ultimate proof that things really are mind over matter.

But I digress.

The point is that Mr. Habsworth was wrong. Money does exist even though he believes otherwise, but as will become clear, this completely wrong belief allowed Mr. Habsworth to become very, very right about something else. He has a tremendous predilection for being both right and wrong at the same time.

Since he did not believe in money, the world confused Mr. Habsworth. Ever since he was a young child he wondered why he could see people doing things that, as far as he was concerned, they had absolutely no reason to do: working jobs, carrying wallets, creating complex financial instruments that gave the recipient regular payments linked to a bundle of home mortgages which were then insured as AAA-backed securities, etc. While people tried to assure him the reasons for these were to make money, to carry money, and because they were idiots respectively, since Mr. Habsworth did not believe in money, he did not believe these explanations. He therefore reasoned that there must be some vast and unseen force that compelled people to do the things they did, one that he as yet could not fathom. He resolved to travel the world to discover this secret reason. This proved to be fairly difficult without believing in money, and turned out to involve a lot of swimming, hitchhiking, and stowing away, but he managed it nevertheless.

First he went to Ethiopia, which at the time was ruled by a group of deeply unpleasant people called the Derg. The Derg had previously ousted the Emperor of Ethiopia (Haile Selassie I) and now ran the country, and although they weren't quite sure what they believed, they were very suspicious of this whole "money" thing that people seemed to keep going on about. From the Derg, Mr. Habsworth learned that governments had tremendous capacity to use force at their disposal, but did not necessarily have to use force to make people do as they pleased. Mr. Habsworth then managed to convince the Derg that there was no such thing as money, which was such an important revelation that the Derg collapsed just a few years later, and were in turn replaced by a wholly different group of deeply unpleasant people, who called themselves something else entirely.

He next travelled to East Asia (that is Travis Habsworth did, not the Derg - they probably would have liked to travel to East Asia if they could but were too busy being shot). There, in East Asia, Mr. Habsworth travelled to the Buddhist monastery on the top of Mt. Falafu, where he stayed for some time. He learned to knife-fight from the Buddhist monks there, but since the Buddhist monks didn't know how to knife-fight he ultimately didn't learn much. He also picked up many of their peculiar habits, with his own alterations. For example, he slept on a bed of one giant spike rather than the many the Buddhists preferred. He also learned much about their spiritual beliefs, about eschewing worldly possessions and achieving enlightenment and so on, but he proved not to be very good at either and left.

Next, he departed for Antarctica. This would prove to be one of his toughest hitchhiking jobs to date but he managed to catch a ride from a friendly passing group of penguins and arrive on the floor of the world, where he saw the wild, unspoiled beauty of nature in all its majestic glory, plus a lot of things penguins did that aren't shown in nature documentaries because they would offend regular people's sensibilities. He travelled to the south pole and felt the sting of the rough, katabatic winds on his cheeks as snow whipped through the air. He stood on the spots where the aforementioned antarctic explorers had conspired to go and contemplated why in the name of any almighty there might be anyone who would ever want to come here (he didn't know about the sled dogs.) He hiked along the Antarctic highway and stealthily observed the scientists of McMurdo station in their natural habitat. After much deliberation, Travis (as the penguins called him) decided that whatever was compelling people to do things must be able to force them to do things they would never think of doing on their own.

Then Travis hitched a ride to San Francisco with the penguins (who were on a beer run) and sat in the DMV for a while. He had told someone in San Francisco that he was getting tired of hitchhiking and he wanted to get a car, so they'd given him a set of instructions that ended in going to the DMV, but all the preceding instructions involved money so he decided to skip right to the end and do the vehicle registration part even though he didn't have a vehicle. So he found the nearest branch of the California Department of Motor Vehicles and was given some forms to fill out, and there, as he waited for hours upon hours in the endless lines and was stonewalled by the grim-faced bureaucrats, he sat down on a bench and had a religious experience. He thought about the Derg and the Buddhist monks and the Antarctic and realized he finally understood what was going on in the world. The entire universe was controlled by paperwork. Paperwork possessed not merely administrative function but in fact direct and vast, perhaps infinite power to affect the nature of the world. Behind all this paperwork there must be bureaucrats. People's lives were being run by a bureaucracy, not a government bureaucracy, but a cosmic bureaucracy, a bureaucracy that instructed people to do all the things he had previously not understood for mysterious and inscrutable reasons of law. He told a clerk about this and he gave Travis more forms to fill out, which in Travis' opinion pretty much confirmed his view of the whole thing. So, in a very roundabout way, Travis had become both right and wrong. He was totally wrong about the money thing, but he had grasped a truth that no one else ever had.

And so he emerged from the DMV an enlightened man, and rolled his eyes upward towards the great government office in the sky and declared that at last he understood.

People nearby ignored him. There were a lot of weirdos in San Francisco.

So Travis Habsworth hatched a plan. He realized that if the world was controlled by paperwork, he could use this to his advantage. Owing to his extremely strange lifestyle, he had never really made any contracts. He would draft his first contract with himself. The contract said, "The undersigned

(Party A) hereby agrees that the undersigned (Party B) will never enter into any other agreement or have any other forms, contracts, paperwork, or bureaucratic instruments of any kind apply to him, and in return Party B agrees to the same provisions."

He signed both dotted lines. And with that agreement with himself, Travis was free. From then on, no contract ever applied to him. None of the forms that ruled the lives of other people meant anything to him any longer. The cosmic bureaucrats, who made other peoples' pens disappear and rocks fall on people's windscreens, didn't have any hold over him. He was immune to paperwork.

The bureaucrats of the next world took note and feared and hated Travis Habsworth, because he was the one person who was beyond their power to influence. His paperwork would never be in order, his forms never in compliance with the required standards, his file never quite full. They would erect a special desk to deal with affairs relating to him and create unique forms revolving around him, but no matter how many forms they signed pertaining to badger attacks and falling bathtubs, nothing ever seemed to affect him. He was the bane of all bureaucracy everywhere, and he threatened the rule of law and good order in the entire universe.

He used this vast power mainly to arrange small piles of twigs into funny shapes, then try to arrange a larger pile of twigs into an even funnier shape, and continue much in the same way until he ran out of twigs. This was very cruel to the twigs, who didn't like being made fun of, but otherwise was relatively benign. The bureaucrats hated him.

And indeed, Travis Habsworth was the only man in the world who could have walked into that nuthouse on the first floor of the Dead Donkey Milton Prodmany Center, Psychology Department, and torn up a Form 21B duly signed and initialed, as Nathan's was. And yet this was exactly what he did.

Chapter 20

Ian stared at the fragments of ripped paper and gibbered.

"Y-you can't do that," he said. "This is most irregular. I will have to report it to my supervisor."

And with that he produced a form, filled it out in duplicate, and popped out of existence.

Nathan watched him feeling that he'd missed something very important.

"I have your form," Travis told him. "Your real form. It says that you're not insane, just very, very strange."

"Oh good," Nathan said happily, and pocketed the form. "Thank you very much, Mr. Habsworth."

"Please, call me Travis. That's what all penguins call me."

Nathan rubbed his feet together and tilted his head in confusion.

"What do you mean penguins?"

"Never mind. Ah, I see your friend has finished his phone conversation."

Brian walked back into the room and frowned at Travis.

"You," he said. His tone was accusatory.

"Me," Travis agreed. "I am Travis Erwin Habsworth, of 2388 Shillington Road, Albany."

"Is this 2388 Shillington Road, Albany?" Brian demanded.

"No."

"Then what are you doing here?"

"I came here to disrupt your evil plans to trick this innocent man into signing a contract against his will." He gestured to Nathan.

Nathan was barely listening; the jingle had started up in his head again.

"I had just gotten a phone call saying that Ian was going to - induce - Nathan to sign his forms, but that you were on the way to stop him."

"Ah. Why didn't you stop me?"

"I did not receive the proper forms. I needed a 937832 - Authorization To Intervene In An Incident Involving Travis Erwin Habsworth."

"I see," Travis said with a nod. "Let this be a lesson to you, Nathan. The principal weakness of the bureaucracy is its inefficiency."

Nathan still wasn't listening. The jingle had just gotten to the best part.

"We have to get you out of here," Travis said to Nathan. "Due to the circumstances surrounding your repeated deaths, you have the capacity to become an even more revolutionary figure than me."

Nathan's jingle ended.

"Oh. That sounds important," he said brightly. "What should I do?"

Travis checked his watch, which was in such bad shape that it looked like he'd stolen it from a hobo.

"I stole it from a hobo," Travis explained as he checked it. "I suggest we go get some afternoon coffee. There is a coffee shop I like downtown. Let's go."

He led them out of the laboratory. They exited the building, interrupted only briefly by Dr. Vegatillius, who was trying to lug Nathan's previous dead body into a room labelled "Musical Studies."

"I have my eye on you," Brian warned Travis as they walked off the university campus. "You won't get away with this. Director Fulcher won't stand for it."

"He will have to stand for it," Travis said calmly. "The bureaucrats," he confided in Nathan, "have vast power. I would go so far as to say that they have infinite power. However, they can only use it in conformity with the universal laws, of which they are the executors. Therefore, they - at the same time - have virtually no power whatsoever. Do you see what I mean?"

"Not at all," Nathan said cheerily.

"Take gravity, for instance. Gravity causes objects to fall to Earth. Every such instance of an object falling to Earth requires paperwork. The bureaucrats who control reality could refuse to file this paperwork and then objects would not fall, but the law instructs that they must file the gravity forms. In a sense their whole purpose for existing is to fill out the gravity forms. Thus they have vast power and at the same time none at all. Do you see?"

Nathan wasn't listening again. They had just rounded a corner to find a half dozen men beating a single man on the ground with hefty sticks.

"Are you playing Muleball?" Nathan asked, remembering the last time they had seen this.

"Oh no, I'm just being mugged," the man on the ground said. "Don't mind me."

One of the muggers approached Travis.

"Give us your money," he demanded.

"I'm sorry. Money doesn't exist," Travis said apologetically. He gave the mugger a sympathetic pat on the shoulder and walked on.

"We shouldn't be with this man," Brian hissed to Nathan. "You don't know him. He's an anarchist. A dissident. A madman. He put the entire legal department into complete disarray. I heard that he once exited the country without a passport or a visa."

"The critical thing to understand is that all paperwork is simply a manifestation of bureaucracy," Travis said calmly. "That is what I have come to realize."

"I parked somewhere around here," Nathan said suddenly.

He wandered around until he found the car he'd borrowed from his neighbor, quickly broke into it, and drove off. Travis gave him directions on where to go. Though the directions were very strange like, "go a block forward, then a block back," and "close your eyes and turn left," Nathan suddenly found that he was sitting in front of a small coffee shop in downtown Dead Donkey that he had never seen before.

Brian's expression darkened, but he said nothing. He had a strange gleam in his eye.

The three men got out of the car and went into the coffee shop.

It was unlike any of the coffee shops Nathan had been in before. There were several small, trendy tables, and Nathan sat down at one. A blonde waitress walked up to them.

"Hello and welcome," she said brightly. "Can I get you something?"

"Nothing for me," Brian said stiffly.

Nathan squinted at the menu of coffee and pastries. He had expected the prices to be highway robbery, but instead they were figures he associated with the prices of Burmese penny stocks.

"I'd like some kind of coffee and a bagel, I suppose," he said.

"Of course, hun," the waitress said, scratching it down. "And for you?" she asked Travis.

"I'd like a coffee as black as-" (what he uttered next

reached a level of racism so shocking it would have made even the whitest veterans of the Rhodesian Bush War blush.)

"One black coffee, coming up," the waitress said awkwardly, and turned and walked away.

Brian and Nathan were staring at Travis, stunned.

"Have I mentioned that I've been to Ethiopia?" Travis said calmly.

The waitress quickly returned.

"Coffee for you two and a bagel for you dear," she said to Nathan, smiling at him.

Nathan thanked her and started to nibble on his bagel.

"Now, down to business," Travis said as he sipped his black coffee. "We need to get you out of the city, Nathan."

"Why?"

"Well, for a start, it's not a very nice city."

"I disagree," Nathan said, looking out the cafe window at the scenic arson across the street.

"Yes, well, it also has someone in it who is trying to kill you. Somehow, the serial killer who murdered you twice has learned that you are still alive, and he is determined to finish you."

"Oh good," Nathan said cheerily. "I think he'd be very disappointed if he told everyone he'd killed me, then found out later that he was wrong. It would be very embarrassing for him. He was such a nice serial killer."

"I believe the man you have just described as 'such a nice serial killer,' has a million-dollar reward associated with him, pooled by the various members of his victims' families and several police departments," Brian piped in.

"Does he get the reward if he kills enough people?" Nathan asked.

Travis held his head in his hands.

Nathan started to sip the coffee. It was coffee in approximately the same sense that asbestos is a food, or bongo player is a job. On the plus side, Nathan felt it would serve very well as a laundry detergent. Remembering that he still hadn't done his laundry, he asked for his coffee to go.

"There you go, dear," the waitress said sympathetically as she handed the coffee to Nathan in a little cardboard cup and tray. He thanked her.

Meanwhile, Travis had recovered and went back to sipping his coffee as if it were a liquid, which it decidedly wasn't. In fact, it was a previously unobserved form of matter called a Bose-Einstein condensate, but since there's never a physicist around when you need one, it would remain unobserved for another fifty-three years, at which time the Dead Donkey physics department head would wander (very drunk) into this cafe one night and order something to drink.

Brian was silently playing a game that bureaucrats like to play when they're out, wherein he mentally documented the number of reportable zoning, labor, and health code violations that he could see from where he was sitting. So far he'd spotted three hundred and thirty four. While he would have liked to get some forms out of his satchel and start writing them all down, the point of the game was to fill out as much paperwork in one's own mind as possible without resorting to pen and paper. If he'd gotten out some forms it would have ruined the fun.

Nathan had forgotten why they'd come here and for some few minutes quite happily thought about his laundry. He had the colored load and the white load, but he suspected he would have to put the white load in with some bleach because of how bloodstained it had all gotten, owing to today's events. Still, he was sure he'd read something about how you get blood out with white vinegar, so it would probably be alright.

Travis coughed to get his attention.

"The point is that since you have died and come back to life so many times, you are an entirely unique person in the entire history of bureaucracy, Nathan. In that respect you are much like myself. But unlike me, the bureaucrats can utterly destroy you by tricking you into signing your missing form, so it is critically important that we get you to some safe place away from the city. Otherwise your life will be in grave danger."

"Good, I'll stay here," Nathan said.

"Your life will be in grave danger!" Travis repeated. "The bureaucrats will eventually induce you to sign the form and then the serial killer will track you down and murder you. Don't you see?"

"Take care of this when you're ready," the waitress said suddenly. She'd sneaked up on them from behind with her painted nails clutching the bill, which she handed to Travis. "It'll be $6.80."

"I'm sorry, money doesn't exist," Travis informed her. He handed her three little pieces of string and a picture of a cat.

The waitress stared at them, then turned to Nathan expectantly. He was fairly sure that he'd left his wallet in his trouser pocket three corpses ago, but he patted himself down and surprisingly found it exactly where it was supposed to be. Nathan fished it out, slapped down his credit card, and waited.

"You have a credit card?" Brian said to Nathan with surprise.

"Oh, it's not mine," Nathan said cheerily. "I take them off the dead salesman that Mr. Fletcher guns down back on my street. Then I use them until they stop working."

"We have to get you out of the city and away from the bureaucrats," Travis insisted. "They will be flooding the place by now, and their administrative cunning knows no bounds except those defined by statute."

The waitress brought the check and Nathan's card back. Nathan picked up the pen and moved to sign it.

"No!" Travis cried, and leapt across the table. "It's a trick."

"What do you mean?" Nathan asked. "I'm just paying... for our..."

He suddenly realized that the blonde waitress with the painted nails looked extremely familiar.

"You!" he said suddenly. "Donna!"

Her face contorted into a look of managerial fury. "How did you know?" she said.

"Well, for a start, you haven't changed your face or hair or nails," Nathan said.

Donna scowled. "I will see you again, Mr. Haynes. And next time I will get you." She reached into her bib pocket and pulled out a form, which she hurriedly initialed. Then she dissolved into nothing.

Nathan blinked and went back to sipping his coffee.

"Do you see?" Travis said. "Their spies are everywhere."

"Brian is a bureaucratic spy," Nathan said calmly. "He keeps following me."

Brian regarded them with a mercilessly bureaucratic stare. It was the kind of look that sent shivers up and down your spine.

"Yes, but that's not my point. They have to trick you into signing the form. They'll try to catch you off your guard, and if you're not careful they will succeed. Then it'll be curtains for you! We have to get you out of here. I've set up a safe house in

Albany."

"But that's very far away," Nathan protested. "Why can't I just stay here and go to sleep? I'm very sleepy. This has been an extremely active day for me."

"We have to go," Travis insisted.

"Oh, very well," Nathan said with a shrug. "I guess the fastest way to get to Albany would be to go to the airport."

For some reason, Travis looked very unhappy with this suggestion, but he shrugged his shoulders and sighed.

"If that's what it takes to get you out of the city, then fine, let's go to the airport."

"I'll drive home and get my things," Nathan said.

"No time. Let's go."

Travis grabbed him by the arm and guided him back into the car.

Nathan did drive to the airport, but he wasn't particularly happy about it.

"I don't see why it would be such a bad thing if I died," he complained. "I mean, it's a bit of a nuisance and I don't really like Director Fulcher shouting at me all the time, but I'll just come back again."

"I've tried to explain. It's not the dying that's important. It's that the bureaucrats will eventually get you to sign a form, then the serial killer will finish you off." Travis frowned. "I have been following all these proceedings with my twigs."

"Hmm?"

"My twigs - I can use them - nevermind, I'll explain later. But there is something very odd about all this. Let's just focus on getting to the airport."

In the back seat, Brian was smiling. Bureaucrats like airports. There is an immense amount of bureaucracy involved with flying, from the ticket to the boarding pass to the security checks to those signs that remind you how much liquid you can take on board. And no smoking signs and seatbelts and instructions from flight attendants - and FAA aircraft standards and electronic device notices and glorious baggage weight restrictions! Everyone complies with all of them. Where else can you wait in line to present a piece of paper to get in the line that demands people remove aspects of their clothing to enter a waiting area to receive another piece of paper? An airport is, therefore, very, very close to a bureaucrats' paradise, except that bureaucrats sometimes have to get places in a hurry too, in which case it's just as much a nightmare for them. As Brian was not in much of a hurry right now, he was smiling.

However, when they finally got to their destination, Brian was wholly unprepared for - and subsequently horrified by - the state of Dead Donkey's airport. First, there were no glorious lines, no security checks, no removal of shoes and jackets to receive a statutory scan or uncomfortable poke with a metal stick. The Transportation Security Administration did not administer security checks on Dead Donkey flights, reasoning that any terrorist would have blown himself up simply from passing through Dead Donkey, long before he got to the airport.

Second, there were no impersonal arrival and departure boards filled with friendly little red LEDs that winked at you and told you whether your flight had been cancelled or merely delayed. This was because Dead Donkey airport was not, strictly speaking, capable of landing large jet liners. Officially, this was because Dead Donkey's runway was not long enough - but this allegation was not entirely accurate. Dead Donkey's runway was more than long enough to accommodate any jetliner that the handful of companies that built such things had yet to design or even conceive of.

The problem dated back to construction. The city of Dead Donkey had always wanted an airport, as the city council had dreamed of luring passenger flights to the city so they could charge them to leave again. But there wasn't enough room in the city of Dead Donkey itself to build the runway, so they had decided to build it underground. Dead Donkey's incredibly massive runway therefore ran underneath the city, with a little slanty-uppy bit at the end for airplanes to leave. Consequently, takeoffs and landings could be a bit tricky in Dead Donkey.

For some reason, commercial airlines refused to service the city of Dead Donkey, even when Dead Donkey had launched its well-publicized campaign to subsidize hijackings to Dead Donkey Intranational Airport. The only people who ever flew out of Dead Donkey were people who had been certified as completely sane by the University Psychology Department, a group of grizzled, bearded, weatherbeaten daredevils in leather flying jackets with prosthetic ears and glasses so heavily mirrored they couldn't see what they were doing. They stood in the lobby of the airport and held up signs with the names of places they wanted to go on them, waiting for passengers to come join them to help subsidize the fuel costs for their elaborately staged suicides.

Nathan walked up to a man who was smoking a cigar the approximate size of Fidel Castro's arm. He had an eyepatch over his left nostril and he was wearing a pistol holster with a large stuffed weasel in it, but what had drawn Nathan to him were the words "NEW YORK," written on his cardboard placard.

"Can you take us to Albany?" Nathan asked cheerily.

The man chewed on the end of his cigarette, then puffed some rancid smoke in their faces.

"I can," he said with a little cough. "The price is a hundred dollars a seat."

Nathan checked his pockets. Then he realized he was still holding the cup of coffee from the cafe and decided to do some savvy haggling.

"I can give you this cup of coffee instead."

The cigar-smoking pilot peered into the murky liquid and took a sip of it. He nodded.

"This'll make good fuel," he said. "I can already taste the lead additive. You've got yourself a deal, stranger. Is it just these three people?"

"I guess so," Nathan said. "I don't really want this one to come." He pointed at Brian.

"Well that's okay," the pilot said. "We'll kick him off somewhere in the middle. Come on, I'll show you out to my plane."

He guided them through the steel maze of the airport into the underground bunker-hanger where Dead Donkey's planes were kept before taxi-ing out onto the runway.

"Here it is," the pilot said, patting it proudly. "My plane. The *Flying Trashcan.*"

Though Nathan was no expert in airplanes, he was not entirely confident of the *Flying Trashcan*'s airworthiness. Maybe it was because it had an odd number of wings, or the fact that its propellers were clearly made out of floppy rubber rather than wood or metal, or that it had little icons of dead passengers stamped on the side like Luftwaffe fighters, but Nathan didn't entirely trust the aircraft. Still, he wasn't a pilot, and he supposed the pilot knew better than he did. It was a lot larger than he expected too. Maybe it could have held thirty people, and surely they wouldn't have let the pilot have such a big airplane if he didn't know what he was doing.

The pilot strapped on his leather flying helmet and pulled down his goggles, stubbed his cigar against the side of the plane, and thwacked the ashes out of his graying beard.

"Alright, let's do this," he said. He knocked on the hatch.

A uniformed female flight attendant opened it from inside. Her makeup was impeccable.

"Hello Captain," she said brightly.

Brian goggled at her in disbelief for a second before allowing himself to be shown in and seated in the front row. There were about twenty seats inside but they were all empty except for the ones the three of them had chosen.

The pilot clambered into the cockpit but kept the door open. There was no co-pilot.

"It's a good thing you folks came along," he said, "it's not economical to fly out to New York without passengers. I've been waiting for weeks."

"Why didn't you just drive?" Brian called up to him.

"Oh, I can't do that," the pilot called back. "I failed my driving test."

He began to flip switches and fiddle with the yoke.

"Now how do you do this again?" he wondered aloud.

After a few experimental prods at some colorful buttons, the aircraft rumbled to life. The pilot taxied out of the hangar and on to the underground runway. As he went, the stewardess began to give her pre-flight briefing.

"Welcome to our nonstop flight to Albany from Dead Donkey, estimated flight time is however long it takes us. Please keep your arms and legs inside the aircraft at all times.

This is a mandatory smoking flight. If you do not have a cigarette, please let your stewardess know and she will provide you with one. Would any hijackers aboard this afternoon please raise their hands?"

She paused. No one raised their hands.

"And now for the in flight safety briefing. In the event of a problem during flight, the pilot will notify us by turning on the emergency situation sign." She gestured to a darkened sign with a picture of a man screaming on it. "This is a signal to put on your vests in the event of a water landing. You will find your vests underneath your seat."

Brian fished under his seat for his vest and pulled it up. It was a skier's jacket.

The flight attendant continued her safety briefing.

"Due to our legal status in several states and countries, we may take anti-aircraft fire during the flight. In the event that shrapnel pierces the canopy, attempt to minimize your cross-sectional area by assuming the brace position, and staunch any bleeding by applying heavy pressure. It may become necessary to jettison the baggage mid-flight, in which case you will unfortunately lose your check-in bags. Our landing in Albany may be 'hot,' and you will have to disembark the aircraft before law enforcement arrives. We understand that you have a choice in airlines and would like to thank you for flying with us."

There was a lengthy silence when she finished.

The aircraft sped down the runway until it got to the slanty bit at the end, through which they could see daylight. The pilot whooped and the *Flying Trashcan* leapt into the air after it cleared the slant. They were in the sky.

The stewardess started to push a cart full of drinks down

the isle, which was not very far since they were all seated in the front row.

"Can I get you anything to drink?" she asked.

Travis shook his head.

"Nothing," Brian said.

"Coffee for me, please," Nathan asked. She gave him an iced coffee, which he sipped happily.

As he did this, the captain shouted back from the cockpit, "which way is New York again?"

"East, captain," the stewardess called back.

"And which way is east again?" he asked.

"Away from the sun," she advised him.

"Oh right."

There was a brief silence.

"What's that big thing in front of us?" he asked.

The stewardess went into the cockpit to consult with him.

"The ground," she concluded. "You want to go away from that."

"Yes, I remember now," he said. The plane veered sharply.

The stewardess pressed a button and a little television monitor descended from the ceiling.

"Our in flight movie is *Oh The Humanity: The Hindenberg Documentary,*" she informed them.

The plane went through a patch of turbulence. At least, Brian hoped it was turbulence.

The waitress came back with a few menus and passed them out.

"We will be serving dinner on this flight," she told them. "You have a choice of steak and rice or the vegetarian option, tofu pot pie with caesar salad. There is a choice of several sides."

"Thank you," Nathan said. He opened the menu and started looking over it. Meanwhile, Brian and Travis watched the documentary, which seemed to be looping footage of the *Hindenberg*'s crash over and over again in ultra-ultra high definition.

"Could you possibly put something else on?" Brian asked after it showed this for the thirtieth or fortieth time. "Maybe something a little more humorous?"

"As it happens, we do have another movie," the flight attendant said. "I've been told it's funny. Would you like me to put that on?"

"Alright," Brian said. "What is it?"

"*Snakes on a Plane.*"

"Some of these desserts look very tasty," Nathan said, staring at a picture of a cupcake on the menu. "I enjoy flying."

"I don't enjoy this flight at all," Brian said coldly.

"Oh, that's too bad. What about you, Travis?"

"I don't believe in flying," he said stiffly. "I do not believe aircraft can fly."

"Then what are we doing right now?" Brian asked him.

"Falling."

Travis Erwin Habsworth had an immense talent for being both right and wrong at the same time, and this instance was a perfect example of that talent. He was wrong because airplanes can fly. He was right because they were, in fact, falling.

Chapter 21

It just so happened that in a classroom not too terribly far from Dead Donkey, a teacher was attempting to explain to a class that airplanes stay up due to a scientific law called Bernoulli's Principle, which is very tricky to understand and often misstated.

The teacher in this particular classroom was explaining that airplanes can stay in the air because the pressure under the wing is greater than the pressure over the wing, thereby creating a net up force on the wing. The net up force on the wing is due to Bernoulli's Principle, which says that air moves faster in low pressure regions. This, the teacher explained, is because air in a relatively low pressure region is by definition moving from a high pressure region, meaning the air is being pushed-

A student raised his hand and asked but what if the air is moving from a lower pressure region into the low pressure region? Then, he reasoned, wouldn't it be in a low pressure region but moving slowly?

At this point the teacher reached over and grabbed a tool he used for dealing with smart-aleck kids who asked tricky questions. It was a heavy stone tipped cane that he called "the Educator," and he used it to strike a firm blow on the head of the student who had asked the question, causing the student to take a brief nap and allowing the teacher to continue with the lecture.

Right, he said, so the point was that air is pushed from the high pressure region into the low pressure region, at which point it is moving fast. So air in low pressure regions is faster than air in high pressure regions. So if the air is moving faster over the wing than beneath it, the air under the wing must be exerting a higher pressure up than the air above the wing is down, and therefore the airplane can fly.

But, asked the student, now recovering from the solid crack to the head, does that just mean any fast-moving air will do? If so, why don't they mount engines over the wings so they can control how fast the air goes over it? Or why wouldn't they put big metal flaps beneath the wings to trap air there, so it moves really slowly-

The teacher gave him another dose of The Educator and he took a short nap.

So, the teacher continued, the point is that wings on airplanes are cleverly designed so that air moves over the wing faster than it moves under the wing, so the pressure will be lower over the wing and so on. This took advantage of something called the equal transit time theory. Basically, the teacher explained, air had to be able to pass the same distance over and under the wing in the same amount of time, because the airplane was only moving at one speed. The airplane's wing was shaped such that there was a curvy, bulgy part on the top of the wing, which in turn forced the air to move faster over the top of the wing to travel the same distance in the same amount of time as the air under the bottom of the wing. And this, he said (with the self-satisfied, smug, knowing grin of someone who has just explained something to a captive audience of children) is why airplanes stay-

One of the first student's friends raised his hand. But if that was really true, he asked, why could airplanes fly upside down? He was pretty sure airplanes could fly upside-down. He'd been to an airshow with his aunt and uncle and seen pilots flying their planes the wrong way round and everything.

A third student piped in that he'd opened their textbook to the section on the history of flight and it showed a picture of the Wright Brother's plane. The wings of the Wright Flyer, he complained, were completely flat. How did it fly?

And what about biplanes? Someone else remembered biplanes. They had flat wings too. How could the pressure above the lower wing be lower than below the lower wing, but higher than above the upper wing? After all, both wings were going at the same speed.

A fifth asked about planes that didn't have wings. He remembered seeing a news article about how NASA was working on something called a lifting body, which could stay in the air even though it didn't have wings at all.

The teacher's fingers were drumming to the tune of the Battle Hymn of the Republic on the handle of The Educator, and he gave all of the students who had spoken up a good, hard thwacking. But by this time a bunch of other students had gotten out their smartphones and were looking at videos on the internet of laboratory dye studies demonstrating that the equal transit time explanation was wrong, and that air did not in fact move over and under the wing in the same amount of time and it all had to do with circulating currents in the reference frame of the aircraft and the obstacle effect. As it so happened, the equal transit time explanation - which was mandated by their school's curriculum - was wrong. It's okay, though. It wasn't a very good school.

Confronted with this rebellion, the teacher told them in a grim deadpan sort of a voice that they would be tested on everything he'd lectured on here today and they'd better darn well know it word-perfect come the exam. Then he whacked them all to sleep and smashed their fancy smartphones.

Unfortunately, Mr. Travis Erwin Habsworth had never attended a class like this, or he would have known better than to say that he didn't believe planes could fly, because it would have earned him a damn good thrashing.

All the students learned an important lesson that day, which was that you shouldn't argue with a man with a heavy wooden stick. Sadly, they had yet to do their lesson on Teddy Roosevelt and therefore hadn't learned this in time to save themselves a lot of napping.

Fortunately for them, though, they would never have to take the test that their teacher had threatened them with, because just after they all left school for home to do their homework and raid their Advil supplies, the *Flying Trashcan* crashed into the schoolhouse, taking the teacher, and The Educator, with it.

Which all just goes to show you that you shouldn't believe everything you learn in school.

Chapter 22

Brian started screaming as the airplane plunged towards the ground.

"It's okay," the pilot shouted from the cockpit. "I'm aiming for that school!"

The airplane was making a loud screeching noise. The engine sputtered and died and there was a sickening wrenching sound as one of the odd number of wings ripped off and careened past their window.

"I think I'm ready to order," Nathan said happily. "I'll have the steak."

The stewardess got up from her seat to take his order. This unto and of itself was an impressive feat, since the g-forces they were pulling were threatening to toss her around like a ragdoll, but the key to working in the service industry is to maintain composure at all times.

"What would you like to drink with that?" she asked him kindly.

"Do you have coke?"

"Pepsi okay?"

"Sure."

Brian continued to scream incoherently.

"I'd like the chocolate mousse for dessert," Nathan added. "And a side salad if you have them."

Travis watched this impassively from his seat.

"This is why I didn't think it was a good idea to go to the airport," he said briefly.

"Would you like anything?" the flight attendant asked him.

"No thank you," Travis said politely. "I'm not hungry at the moment."

Brian was still screaming.

In the cockpit, the pilot was wrestling with the controls, which did nothing to increase Brian's confidence in him. He was fairly sure that you were supposed to work the pedals with your feet and the yoke with your hands, rather than what the pilot was doing. Smoke was filling the cockpit (not because the plane was on fire; the pilot was still smoking) and Brian was fairly certain that some of the things ripping off the airframe were quite important to their continued airworthiness.

He screamed and screamed.

"It's okay!" the pilot shouted back from the cockpit to reassure him. "Look on the bright side. The flight's gonna be a lot shorter than you thought."

The stewardess re-emerged from the kitchen area and handed Nathan a salad and can of cola. Nathan opened the can and most of the liquid spilled out due to the funny sort of spin that the plane was doing now.

"Just try to think of this as a very exciting landing," the pilot shouted back from the cockpit.

"Shouldn't you be radioing for help?" Travis asked. He believed in radios.

"What?"

"The radio," Travis said calmly. "Shouldn't you be using it?"

"What's a radio?" the pilot shouted back.

"Or shouldn't you at least be lowering the landing gear?" Travis inquired, though he admitted this was a bit on the optimistic side.

"Oh, I don't have any of that stuff," Travis said. "We never had any to begin with. The maintenance costs - you wouldn't believe them - just for a bunch of wheels?"

Brian stopped screaming. He had passed out from fear.

The ground was getting bigger and bigger. Nathan watched it with a sort of vague interest as he munched on his salad. The cereal jingle was playing in his head again.

"Are you sure you wouldn't like any salad?" he asked Travis. "You look like you might be a little hungry."

"I'm fine, but thank you," Travis said politely.

"Just a bite. You should try it. It's very good salad."

"Oh, fine. Just a bite."

Then they hit the ground, whereupon the schoolhouse the pilot was aiming at and the *Flying Trashcan* rather violently became the same object.

Chapter 23

Suddenly, Nathan found himself standing in a void of big, black nothing behind the stewardess, the pilot, and a school teacher he had never met before. The school teacher was carrying a very large beating stick. Brian and Travis were nowhere to be seen.

"Where are we?" the pilot said in obvious confusion and consternation. "Is this heaven?"

"You have just deliberately piloted an airplane into a school," his stewardess reminded him. "Do you really think we are in heaven?"

"Yes?" he asked uncertainly.

"Station Number Four, please," the loudspeaker voice rang out, and the frumpy woman materialized. She peered unhappily at Nathan.

"You. Fulcher's office now. Director's orders," she said. The exit door appeared.

"Thank you," he said. Before he went he turned to the three people in line ahead of him. "If you want my advice," he said confidentially, "don't sign the 21B."

The frumpy woman scowled at him.

About a minute later, Nathan was again seated in Director Fulcher's familiar office.

"Have you changed the furniture around?" Nathan asked cheerily, looking at the alternating line of seats and potted plants. "I thought it went seat-seat-seat-plant, but now it's seat-plant-"

"The furniture is immaterial," Director Fulcher said cooly. This was in fact one of the least accurate statements he had made today, but he was so frustrated he wasn't very fussed about it.) "I understand that you have not only died again, but you have also come into contact with Mr. Travis Erwin Habsworth. Is that right?"

"Yes," Nathan confirmed. "We had coffee together."

"Your papers become less and less in order by the minute. I must advise you, Mr. Haynes, that there are few men alive less trustworthy than Mr. Habsworth. He does not believe in law, or structure, or bureaucratic execution of statutes."

"I think he does believe in all that. He doesn't believe in airplanes though. He told me so."

"If he sought you out to make contact, he is probably just using you towards some hideous and unknowable end. Who knows what dark purpose he intends to direct you towards! Back away now, Mr. Haynes. Sign your 21B."

"No, I don't think I will," Nathan said. "Oh, and that reminds me. I want to give you this."

He passed him the note from the psychologist.

"It says I am not insane."

"It says you were charged $6.80 for several cups of coffee and a bagel," Director Fulcher said, reading it.

"Oh, right, sorry," Nathan said apologetically. "This is the one that says I'm not insane."

Fulcher inspected it with a frown. "It is true that with this added to your file, I will have great difficulty in declaring you insane, although I maintain that the fact that you have now died... What is it? Four times today... speaks for itself."

"I don't think any of them were really my fault," Nathan said. "Badger attacks can happen to anyone. Besides, I quite enjoy dying. You have a lovely office."

"The loveliness of my office is not at issue here," Fulcher snapped. He quickly stowed a little doily he was using as a coaster back in its drawer. "The point is that you must eventually sign your 21B and remain here after death! It is mandatory!"

"But that doesn't mean I have to do it," Nathan argued.

"That is exactly what it means!"

"I know that you've sent Brian, Ian, and Donna after me already."

"Yes. I was most displeased that Donna failed to obtain your signature. I'm sure you have realized by now that it was I who put your wallet back on your body so you would be compelled to pay for the coffees..."

"Are you going to keep sending bureaucrats to force me to try to sign your form?"

"Yes. Until the job gets done."

"Oh, that's too bad," Nathan said. "You'll probably get very mad at all of them when they fail."

Fulcher's face got very red.

"You have some nerve to come in here and say that to me, Mr. Haynes, I must say... But I will tell you again: I will get your papers in order, no matter what it takes. Goodbye, Mr. Haynes."

And with that he signed some unseen form and Nathan was zapped back to life.

Chapter 24

Everyone alive knows someone who seems to be effortlessly better off than they are. This someone drives a faster car, lives in a bigger house, eats at nicer restaurants, and spends time with more attractive people than the observer. Most frustrating, this someone appears to do no real work but is instead massively overcompensated for having sold stocks at the right time or gone to business school or been born the child of a terminally ill billionaire. Generally, amid a sense of building resentment and hatred, we the observers shake our heads and feel that some people - some immensely unpleasant and undeserving people - have all the luck and the rest of us are stuck with none.

This isn't quite right. Sociologists have attempted to discern why the faster-car, bigger-house, nicer-restaurant-goers (FBNs) exist and have devised a theory of social relativity, stating that all success must be measured relative to the observer but regardless of your success relative to any other object, you still appear to have the same success relative to any FBN. This doesn't make any sense, and in fact is a load of nonsense.

The real reason FBNs exist is that they have bribed the cosmic bureaucrats. The trick to winning at life isn't working hard or staying in school or ruthlessly destroying your enemies, although the last one is immensely satisfying in its own way. Rather, it is to slip a cosmic bureaucrat a few twenties at the right time, ideally shortly before you are born, and then just ride the wave of good fortune that comes your way thereafter. If you manage to find a corruptible bureaucrat, they will be more than happy to push a 5074784 - Authorization To Live A

Charmed Life - your way and then it will be pretty much all uphill for you thereafter. Bureaucrats are generally overworked, underpaid, and unhappy with their jobs and are often quite happy to accept a few bucks in exchange for a favor.

Of course, corruption is a matter of deep concern to the bureaucratic leadership and they have renewed their commitment to stamp it out by forming the Exploratory Committee on the Committee on the Committee on the Committee to Design A Process To Introduce a Form To Deliver Swift Retribution Against Corrupt Personnel, or they would have formed it except the motion got held up in committee. Corruption therefore remains endemic among the bureaucrats of the next world, and they'll help you out if you help them out. A hundred dollars and a few smokes is usually a good starting point, but if you're a clever negotiator you can often get the price down to fifty. Some bureaucrats offer discounts for the whole family.

If Nathan had done this at any of his several opportunities, he would probably have lived a very happy life and not had to worry about any of the things he did now: ie: planes crashing into the ground and badgers breaking into his house and attacks by clowns (which had not happened to him yet but he was very worried about). However, since he lacked that kind of foresight and business acumen, he was stuck always a heartbeat away from the next badger and/or clown attack, which he was starting to regard as very inconvenient.

Chapter 25

"Welcome back," Travis told Nathan when he rematerialized. They were standing in the wreckage of the plane and the school, respectively, the unrecognizable remains of the pilot, stewardess, teacher, Educator, and Nathan's own body somewhere underneath the plane. Bags that certainly weren't theirs were strewn all over the place.

Travis, however, looked totally untouched. He had Brian - also completely unscathed - under one arm. He had Nathan's salad in his free hand, and he was munching on it.

"This is good," he agreed. "You must forgive me - I only had time to save one of you and the salad, so I chose Brian. I thought that he shouldn't have a chance to report back to his superiors if it could at all be avoided."

"But how did you survive?" Nathan asked.

"Laws are merely the invention of bureaucrats and have no power over me. Gravity - death - these things are all in the mind."

"Oh. And New York too?"

"No. New York is real."

"That explains everything," Nathan said with a nod. He looked around in the debris and spotted his can of cola which, although somewhat flatter than it had been previously, was still intact. He picked it up and sipped the remaining dregs of liquid from it.

"It's frothier than before," he commented. "Anyway, what should we do now? It's getting a bit late. Maybe we should go back to my house."

"Your serial killer will be looking for you back at your home. Also, the bureaucrats will expect you to return to Dead

Donkey. We must take you to Albany. I have prepared a safe house for you there."

"How can a house be safe from bureaucrats?"

"I filled it with the things bureaucrats fear. Pink slips. Improperly filed forms. Stern letters from politicians. Electronic form-filing systems that render them obsolete. They will not be able to harm you there. But first we have to get to Albany. We must obtain transport. I would prefer something ground based."

"Well, we could pretend that you're rich. Then the city would give you a car to go away."

"Excuse me?" Travis said politely.

The city of Dead Donkey had a problem a few years ago: owing to a growing urban gentrification movement and dramatically increased popularity of xylophone fences, arson, and dieting spoons, a lot of rich people suddenly started appearing in Dead Donkey. Residents complained that they didn't want the city full of some stuck up rich people who looked down on them, and asked the mayor to get up off his butt and do something about it for once.

The mayor concluded that, logically speaking, the rich people wouldn't leave unless they had a way to leave, and that they therefore needed cars. Following this excellent line of reasoning, he started the Dead Donkey cars 4 rich people program, which came (literally) hot on the heels of the wildly successful flamethrowers 4 arsonists program. However, like the flamethrowers, the program backfired. No matter how many cars the mayor gave to the rich people on the city's dime, they insisted on staying where they were. In fact, a lot of them seemed to be doubling down. As a stopgap measure, the mayor started handing out money with the cars as well, in the hopes that paying the rich people would cause them to go away, but this didn't work either.

The Mayor of Dead Donkey is not very popular.

However, Nathan had no time to explain this to Travis (who would not have understood it anyway since he did not believe in money), because a large red firetruck screeched to a halt not fifteen feet away from them. As soon as it stopped, the siren turned on.

"No you idiot," one of the firefighters clinging to the side shouted, "you're supposed to turn it on before we get here."

Someone inside the engine shouted a muffled apology.

The firefighters clambered off the side of the truck. One rolled out a hose and stared at it skeptically for a moment, then stared down the barrel as if he didn't know exactly how to work it. After he fiddled with the nozzle for a second, a burst of water came out and hit him in the face.

There was a dark laugh from inside the firetruck.

"Idiot!" the laughing voice called. "You're supposed to turn it on, then point it at your face, not point it at your face then turn it on."

"I take it," Travis said quietly, "that this is the Dead Donkey fire department."

"It is," Nathan confirmed.

As the firefighters argued about whether or not they were supposed to water the nearby trees or instead create a circle of water to surround the burning school house, Nathan stood up, dusted himself off, and walked up to them. Travis followed, with the still unconscious Brian under one arm.

"Hello," Nathan said to the nearest firefighter. "Can you take us back to the city?"

"I dunno," the firefighter said dubiously. "My job

description doesn't say anything about rescuing people."

"Maybe you could try it just for a laugh," Travis suggested, sliding Brian into an empty seat in the firetruck. "You might enjoy it."

The firefighters huddled up and discussed this possibility for a second while their little wiener dog ran around yipping at their heels. Travis gave it the bacon bits from his salad and it barked happily as it licked them off the muddy ground (the ground was muddy because the hose was flooding the nearby earth with about a thousand gallons of water).

The circle of firefighters reached a decision after a few minutes of nattering, during which time the aircraft wreckage seemed to have conveniently extinguished itself.

"Alright," one of the firefighters said as the circle broke up. "We'll drive you back to the city. But if our supervisor or anyone else asks, you'll tell them that this was a false alarm. Agreed?"

"Agreed," Nathan said, and piled into the cabin next to Travis and the unconscious Brian.

Chapter 26

The practice of recreational drinking in the city of Dead Donkey has taken a rather unusual turn. Historically, Dead Donkey always had the highest average alcohol consumption per capita in the world but a median alcohol consumption amounting to virtually nothing. What any public policy analyst could tell you, provided they could be bothered to stop burning down the city long enough to do so, was that this meant a very small number of people in the city had a very big alcohol problem. This is because while most of Dead Donkey's various residents found one way or another to cope with the daily horror of living in the city - insanity, criminal activity, blindness, or participation in local government, for example - a small nucleus of Dead Donkey's citizenry relied on alcohol to get them through the day. They were generally regarded as the hardest drinking people in the world, collectively consuming approximately a quizillion units of alcohol a day.

Despite the massive quantity of alcohol consumed, there weren't very many drinkers because for the longest time there was only one bar in the city, and the regulars in this bar didn't take kindly to strangers to such an extent that the only time an outsider had ever had drinks there was once in 1986. His obituary had appeared in the paper the next day.

The aforementioned unusual turn began some years later, when due to worsening terms of trade resulting from the closure of the xylophone fence factory and the mayor's short-lived decision to abandon the US dollar in favor of the Burmese kyat, the price of beer began to skyrocket in Dead Donkey. Eventually, the beer crisis became so bad that the

Dead Donkey drinkers could no longer buy beer for less than the price of the triple-liver-bypass surgeries they relied on to keep themselves alive.

After one morning of particularly terrifying hangovers, the Dead Donkey barflies resolved to do something about the crisis. They tried to make their own alcohol but soon discovered that this required grain, yeast, and preferably sobriety while operating the still, so this endeavor was quickly abandoned. Then they tried to steal beer, but remembered that theirs was the only bar in Dead Donkey and it didn't have any. Then they tried to organize a tontine, but realized none of them knew what a tontine was.

They tried vodka, but decided it tasted terrible, and instead opted for an alternate solution. Recreational drinkers in Dead Donkey now drink a noxious cocktail of battery acid, bitterant, and kerosene called Dead Donkey ale, which they chug down while being pummeled in the head with sticks. Then they sing their favorite songs in slurred voices. This approximately emulates the taste, effect, and experience of drinking actual alcohol, with the added advantage of being less taxing on their internal organs.

Dead Donkey ale is traditionally served with a slice of orange.

Knowing all this, you should be able to understand exactly how dire the situation was when Nathan said, "I think I need a drink."

The firefighters had just dropped them off in the middle of town. They had not taken them all the way to the fire station because they had seen a building burst into flames in the distance, urgently deposited their passengers on the roadside, then quickly slammed the accelerator to the floor and put as much distance between themselves and that fire as possible.

To tell the absolute truth, Nathan was feeling a little bit melancholy. Travis had told him that he couldn't go home, he was a bit on the tired side, and he had died more times than was normal for him. Brian was looking very pale too, so Nathan concluded they needed a drink, and, as it happened, they were just outside the only bar in Dead Donkey: the Lucky Loser. Nathan pushed open the door to the Lucky Loser. Travis followed him with a shrug, Brian still slung over his shoulder.

They walked in and something told Nathan that this was a rough bar.

Maybe it was the large neon sign hanging over the door that said, "This Is A Rough Bar." Or maybe it was the list of people who had died in bar fights pinned to the wall by a bloody knife; the list itself was written in a font size small enough to baffle the cosmic bureaucrats and fell down almost to the floor. Or maybe it was the pool table, which had a roundish skull for a ball.

But the overall impression was that this was not a place you wanted to enter unless you were either prepared to fight your way out again or had realized it was the cheapest alternative to Dead Donkey's airlines to commit an elaborate assisted suicide.

Fortunately for Nathan, no one was inside to brutally murder him, which the regulars surely would have done if they had been here at the moment. The room was totally empty except for a bartender in a surprisingly nice jacket and tie, standing behind a wooden bar counter. Nathan walked up to it and sat down.

"What's your story, fellah?" the bartender asked him. "You look like you've had a rough day."

"I had a stroke and I was attacked by a badger," Nathan said. "To be honest, I think that was the best part of my afternoon."

"You sound like you need a drink," the bartender said. He poured him a significant measure of the brown ambiguous liquid from the tap and slid it over to Nathan. One drop trickled down the side of the glass and promptly burned a hole in the bar.

"Where are all the other customers?" Nathan asked as he contemplated drinking this liquid.

"They're all working their shift."

"Their shift?" Nathan inquired.

"They're all firefighters," the bartender informed him.

"All of them?"

"Well, not all of them. Some of them are arsonists." He started wiping a nearby glass. "You wouldn't believe the mess the bar fights make. What'll you have?" he asked, turning to Travis.

"Nothing," Travis replied. "I just wonder if you could tell me how to get out of this city in a hurry."

The bartender contemplated this as he wiped his glass. "Tricky," he said.

It should be explained that owing to its geographical location, socioeconomic climate, and the fact that no one else in the entire world wants to go to Dead Donkey unless they are completely out of their skulls, there aren't many transport links to and from Dead Donkey. Aircraft can go in and out of Dead Donkey via the airport, provided they don't crash and aren't shot down by the flak batteries that secure the airspace around the city. Dead Donkey has no rail links with the rest of the world, and its one street has such an immense traffic jam in the outgoing direction that many of the commuters have begun to run side businesses out of their cars.

As many people want to escape Dead Donkey, various alternative transport schemes have been tried over the years. The city council once proposed building a seaport, brushing aside objections that the city is in the middle of the desert. Dead Donkey now has the world's largest inland seaport, but the *California Queen* - a supersized cruise ship that is docked in the port - has yet to set sail due to what the captain insists are administrative difficulties and what the US Coast Guard has identified as "sand in the propellers." Some other methods have also been attempted, though they have generally speaking not borne out very well in practice. Tucker Sanchez, a lifetime resident, constructed a giant slingshot and attempted to launch himself towards California but miscalculated the angle and ended up going straight up and then falling straight back down again. His giant slingshot was subsequently appropriated for use in Muleball games. A handful of residents attempted to convince the federal government that there had been an earthquake in Dead Donkey and that military helicopters needed to be sent to evacuate them. While the nation was briefly shocked and horrified by the videos of human suffering that the residents sent them, the US Geological Survey quickly concluded that the little blip on their seismographs had not in fact been an earthquake but about fifty people jumping up and down at the same time. Rescue efforts were subsequently abandoned.

The most successful ever escapee of Dead Donkey was a man named Karenval Hooke, who realized that he could leave the city by simply driving the wrong way down the in road into Dead Donkey, because no one in their right mind ever came into the city and the in road was therefore almost entirely clear. Local legend insists he is still serving the jail sentence he received for reckless driving once he made it to Las Vegas.

"Tricky," the bartender repeated. "The nearest settlement from here is - oh - a hundred miles away, and everything from here to there is unforgiving desert. Just vast endless sands, cactus, and roadside McDonalds, as far as the eye can see. You'd have to be crazy to try. Have you tried riding out on horseback?" He suggested. "The horse would have to be bribed, of course, but you might be able to convince it to make the attempt."

Nathan was still staring at his drink; he'd hadn't tasted it yet, but the fumes were causing his nostrils to bleed.

"I have been killed by a serial killer twice and died in a plane crash once, and I still haven't done my laundry," he complained. "Bureaucrats are after me and all the riding in the firetruck made me feel carsick. That's why I felt I needed a drink."

Travis ignored him.

"When I was traveling in Africa," he said, "I learned that I do not get along very well with horses."

"How can you tell?" Nathan asked.

"Mainly because they kept walking off the road and taking me into graveyards. I got the message after the twentieth time it happened."

"What did you do to make the horses so mad at you?"

"I think it probably has to do with my smell," Travis said with a shrug. "And because at the time I was working as a glue salesman."

"I thought you didn't believe in money."

"I don't," Travis said airily. "I still believe in work. That is the point."

Nathan didn't entirely follow, but then again he had taken a sip of the Dead Donkey ale, and everything had gone quite hazy.

"Why is the room suddenly so foggy?," he asked Travis. "Did you turn on a cloud machine? Please stop it."

Travis ignored him.

"Is there any other way out of the city?" he asked.

The bartender thought about this, and then shrugged his shoulders.

"If you can't drive - if you already tried flying - if you're not willing to ride - there's only one way out of Dead Donkey." He leaned in confidentially. "You'll have to go to a travel agency. They'll work in an emergency. But it'll cost you."

"That's alright," Travis said. "I don't believe in money."

"And I don't believe in drinking, but I still work here," the bartender said with a shrug.

Nathan had taken another sip of the ale and staggered. He pushed it away, deciding it was not to his liking.

Brian stirred groggily.

"Oh no," he said, looking around. "Why am I awake? I preferred things the other way."

"Drink this," Nathan advised him.

He took a sip and immediately jumped up as if he'd sat on an angry cat. Travis hauled Brian to his feet, thanked the bartender, and went to leave - Brian in tow.

"I'm afraid you'll have to pour the rest of this out," Nathan advised the bartender.

The bartender shrugged and poured it down the sink. The sink melted.

They walked back outside into the late afternoon cool.

"You know," Travis commented suddenly, "Dead Donkey is a very violent place."

"Is it?" Nathan asked as a car bomb exploded in the distance. "I've never noticed."

"Yes, it is," Travis affirmed. Just across the street three masked men had confronted an old lady in a flagrant mugging in broad daylight. It was over in a heartbeat; the three masked men were left unconscious on the roadside and the old lady walked away whistling, their wallets clutched in her gnarled hands.

On the street corner, a disgusting hobo was sitting surrounded by filth, clad in scummy gray rags. His gnarled hands grasped a cardboard sign that said, "please help," in permanent marker. Despite the apparent direness of his situation, he was laughing, periodically taking a few swigs from a steel flask of ale. His dirty face glowed with delight as he did this and he muttered nonsense words, his wild eyes jumping between pedestrians.

Brian stopped to stare at him.

"Look at that man," he said, indicating the hobo.

Nathan briefly glanced at him and nodded thoughtfully.

"You know, I think that's the happiest I've ever seen the mayor."

Chapter 27

The Dead Donkey City Council has long since decided that they're going to be damned if they let anyone improve the city of Dead Donkey more than they have. Since they have never succeeded in improving the city in any way whatsoever, the business of the Dead Donkey City Council now consists mainly of denying building permits (as indeed does the business of most city councils). Like all city councils, they have a vast array of political weasel words that they can use to deny a building permit. If a site is dilapidated and ugly, they can call it "historic." If it is undeveloped and ugly, they can call it "natural." If it is overbuilt and ugly, they can call it "urban."

If, on the other hand, it is beautiful, they can call it "marked for demolition."

Using these clever weasel words, the city council has managed to table all motions for useful construction for the past three decades.

(Coincidentally, owing to the undue influence of vast Swedish furniture cabals in government, all parliamentary procedures are named after types of furniture. A motion is said to be "tabled" if it has been postponed, a committee is said to be "chaired" by its leader, and an elected lawmaking body is said to be "Ottomanned" if it has recently been sidelined by the growing influence of Janissaries. This is also the reason that virtually all lawmaking bodies have suspiciously nice furniture, regardless of how small or irrelevant they actually are.)

This explains why there is only one road going into or out of the city of Dead Donkey, and the outgoing section of this road has a traffic jam that is entering its sixth decade and will shortly become eligible for social security benefits.

The total lack of city development and infrastructure spending means that a tremendous number of people want to leave Dead Donkey, but no one actually can. This has itself contributed to the rise of travel agencies in Dead Donkey.

Travel agencies in Dead Donkey run a business that consists primarily of luring people into the city proper with promises of free transport (there is no traffic jam coming into the city since no one ever wants to come in) and then charging them through the nose to leave. Most are willing to pay the exorbitant prices that these businesses require. If their fee is met, the travel agencies will then transport the traveler in question out of the city with all due haste - no questions asked - though how they go about this is so heavily privileged information that it puts the Colonel's secret blend of spices to shame. Supposedly only one man knows the method by which travel agencies spirit people out of the city, and he is constantly being watched by an assassin whose orders are to shoot him if he ever tells anyone. He lives a rather tense life, as does the assassin, since she herself has another assassin waiting to kill her in case she fails to kill the man with the secret.

Nathan was not thinking about any of this. Rather, he had just seen a piece of thin, bendy plastic sheeting by the roadside and pocketed it, deciding it would be nice to have for later.

Meanwhile, Brian was being brought up to speed.

"So what are we doing now?" he asked.

"Leaving," Travis said matter-of-factly.

"Oh good," Brian said brightly. He was already looking forward to filling out the necessary paperwork to authorize his departure from this wretched hellhole.

Nathan frowned. He quite liked this wretched hellhole.

"I don't really see why I have to go," he said.

Travis raised his eyebrows.

"Someone is trying to kill you in this city."

"But that's not so bad, is it?"

"And Director Fulcher is trying to put your file in order."

"I won't let him."

"Given how close you have already come to letting him trick you..."

"I won't let it happen again."

"Regardless, we need to get you out of here. If our information is correct, the people here should help you to do that."

Travis stopped in front of a heavily fortified metal door. A sign on the front said "Travel Agency."

He knocked on it. A little window slid open in the door, though it was no larger than a slit.

"What's the password?" the man behind the door demanded.

"We want to get out of Dead Donkey," Travis said.

The man blinked at them.

"Password?" Nathan suggested.

"Eh, close enough," he said, and opened the door. "It was hxfpnszumb."

"That's basically the same," Nathan agreed as the bulky guard stood aside to admit them.

Inside, there was a counter much like one would find at an old airport ticket desk. A young man sat behind it.

"Can you take us to Albany?" Travis asked the man.

The man frowned.

"Can I interest you in a trip to Australia?" he asked.

"No. I'd like to go to Albany."

"It's just that I could offer you a very good deal for

Australia right now," the man advised them.

"It's got to be Albany," Travis said insistently.

"Albany, Australia, what's the difference?" the man said urgently. "They're practically the same. Why not go to Australia instead? Who will know?"

Travis raised his eyebrows.

The travel agent misinterpreted this as a positive sign and pressed on.

"You could explain away your tans by saying that you'd visited a tanning salon," he said zealously. "And you could take a picture of yourself in front of the Sydney Opera House and tell your friends it's the New York governor's mansion."

He paused to collect his thoughts.

"You could tell your friends that kangaroos are native to New York."

"I am not going on a vacation," Travis said firmly. "I do not believe in vacations. I must go to Albany, New York, and not to any other place however similar a name it might have."

Not to be deterred, the travel agent said, "Ayer's Rock is basically the same as New York City."

While Nathan was slightly impressed by the zeal with which the man had advocated Australia, and was even starting to come around to his viewpoint a little, Travis held his ground.

"Albany," he said.

"Fine, fine. But I'll have to check with my supervisor. I can only authorize trips to Australia."

"Then please fetch your supervisor."

The young man retreated into the shadows.

There was a reason he had been so insistent about sending them to Australia.

Australia is not, as is commonly believed, a vast, wealthy,

and extremely happy country in the southeastern corner of the globe settled by ex-British convicts who mellowed out considerably and built a fancy opera house once they'd gotten a bit of sun. First of all, globes do not have corners. Second, Australia is in reality a crazed anarchic hellscape where machine-gun toting grizzled Australian troopers are deployed alongside eyepatch-wearing koala infantry to battle ferocious emu warlords and their kangaroo allies. Control of the continent regularly shifts between dictatorial factions as they battle for control of the continent's precious metal and vegemite reserves.

However, the Australians are extremely concerned that all this fighting and looting of natural resources for obscene profit will damage their reputation internationally, so they have gone to great lengths to pretend otherwise. They have heavily subsidized visitation to their country so people can come to tourist destinations like Sydney (in local language the treaty-town of New Wartopia), where tourists wander around and visit the Opera House (the New Politarmy's Conquest Headquarters, on the days when there are no tourists around) and spend money on overpriced souvenirs and then go home and tell their friends how marvelous Australia was. Australia's international reputation is therefore preserved and people don't think of Australians as criminals anymore. Since the man at the counter in the travel agency got a sizable kickback for every person he sent to Australia, he was very well incentivized to make a convincing pitch to that effect.

Travis did not know any of this. He did not believe in Australia.

The first travel agent returned shortly.

"My supervisor says that it's alright, but we don't allow

people to travel in groups. I'll have to admit you to the next room one at a time."

Travis bowed his head in agreement.

"I will go first," he said.

And the man led him away.

Chapter 28

A few minutes later, the travel agent returned and led Nathan deeper into the bowels of the travel agency. Nathan was ultimately deposited alone in a very dark room.

"Hello?" he said.

Dim lights flickered on around him. He was standing in the center of a gunmetal gray platform. A nearby massive shadowy object was looming over him, and just beneath it was a tall man in a nice suit.

"Are you the supervisor?"

"I am," the man confirmed.

"Where's Travis?"

"We have already sent him on to Albany," the supervisor said cooly.

"You have? How?"

The supervisor gave him a cool smile. The dim lights in the room flickered, then suddenly jumped from soft to radiant. The shadowy object in the center of the platform was bathed in light. Nathan squinted at it through the glare. The nearest part of the object seemed to be some kind of pointy, shiny tube that narrowed near the end. The tube was linked by way of a large metal arm to a vast sort of chrome crane-like-structure, coated in wires and antennae, which was itself connected to a customer satisfaction survey.

Nathan stared at it.

"What is that?" he asked uncertainly.

"That," the supervisor said cheerily, "is how you are going to get to Albany. I take it that you don't know what it is?"

Nathan did not know what it was, because he had never seen a teleportation device before.

Quantum physics holds that it is possible for particles to teleport, to diffuse through solid objects, and do a whole lot of other wacky things that most scientists hope they won't have to think about because of how confusing it is. In fact, most scientists secretly think that the quantum physicists belong in the same category as the molecular biologists, cosmologists, and deep sea oceanographers - which is to say that they suspect the quantum physicists have been pulling their legs this whole time and the entire subject is just a scam for grant money. Unfortunately for those scientists who want to have a deterministic view of the universe, the quantum physicists are not in fact pulling their legs and uncertainty is the rule, not the exception.

The gist of quantum physics is that matter's sense of self is all a bit wobbly when you get right down to it. Things aren't really at places, there are only places that they might be (which is the reason you can never find your keys when you are late for work). So long as no one has thought to look, you might be sitting in your chair at home or you might be at work, or you might be somewhere else entirely - say, Albany. Some things are so hard to look at that they are really nowhere at all. This is called the uncertainty principle.

While this was all very exciting, unfortunately it cannot, unto and of itself, be used as a teleportation device, because despite all of the excitement around uncertainty-based revelations, after all the math was done, it turned out you still needed to be moving to go somewhere. This was deeply unfortunate for the community of engineers trying to develop teleportation, but another physics revelation soon brightened their day.

After building a lot of monolithically huge and fantastically expensive atom smashers, which allow particle physicists to slam the foundations of reality together until they break, particle physicists realized that particles are not really particles at all - they are, sort of, waves. This distinction is very difficult to explain to a layman, but basically think of it in terms of tennis balls.

If a particle is a tennis ball, and you are a tennis player, you can hit the particle/tennis ball and it will bounce off your racket, and off the other player's racket, and off the floor and sometimes hit the net and the game can be played as normal.

A wave is like a particle, except sometimes the ball goes through the racket without explanation.

It turns out that particles are not particles at all but rather kinda sorta also waves, which means sometimes they can go through the racket too.

If a person could be turned into a wave, they could travel to say, Albany, very very fast because they would not have to fuss with all the solid objects (traffic jams, mountains, particle colliders, etc.) in between. If they could be accelerated to near the speed of light, this would functionally be teleportation. Unfortunately, there is no known process for turning people into waves.

The critical revelation came when these two ideas were put together, and someone realized that if you were kinda-sorta a wave, that means you *might be a wave*, in which case the trick was to do the opposite of what the particle physicists were doing and pointedly not look at you. If no one was looking at you, then you *might be a wave*, and if you *might be a wave*, you might be wherever you wanted to be, say, Albany.

They simply had to guarantee that no one would look at you. So they had constructed a device that relied on the power of the one object that no one ever looked at: an eighty-four page online tiny screwmaker's customer satisfaction survey, which renders the target of the device effectively invisible to the human psyche and indeed the psyche of most higher mammals. It is the greatest source of boredom and indifference that man has ever known, and it forms the core of teleportation technology.

The rest of it was pretty easy. The trick was to look at yourself when you reached Albany, and then the wavefunction would collapse, etc., and you would be in New York.

Naturally, this device was such a stunning and powerful technological breakthrough that it could only be entrusted to travel agents, who swore to use it only for good. They located it in Dead Donkey, where they used it to help people leave the city (and if that isn't good, nothing is).

Looking at the teleportation machine, Nathan assumed it was putting icing on extremely large cakes. The mere thought immediately made him the third wrongest man alive, behind Stephen Hawking and Travis Erwin Habsworth, and considerably ahead of people who think shaving off their eyebrows makes them more attractive.

"This is a teleportation machine," the supervisor informed Nathan summarily.

"Oh," Nathan said. His musings about who would eat such a large cake and what it might taste like instantly vanished, and he dropped a few billion places down the wrongness charts.

"In a moment I will activate the machine and take you to Albany," the supervisor continued. "But first I need you to agree that you will not disclose the secret of the teleportation device to anyone. Otherwise we get to send you to Australia."

"Alright," Nathan agreed.

"I'll need you to sign this form to that effect," the man said. He crossed to the part of the room where Nathan was standing, in the dim twilight, produced a clipboard with a small form on it, and offered it to Nathan.

Nathan moved to sign it.

"Incidentally," Nathan asked just before he did, "what is that?"

He pointed to the customer satisfaction survey.

The supervisor briefly glanced at it.

"Nothing to worry about. I'm afraid that only one person in the whole world knows exactly how this device works and he is not here."

"Oh. It looked like a customer satisfaction survey to me."

Nathan signed the form, and the supervisor quickly countersigned.

The moment he did so, Nathan recognized several important points about the supervisor. He was about six and a half feet tall. His hair was a formidable brown-gray, and his eyes were dark and totally merciless. He was not wearing a tie.

Director Fulcher whooped and snatched the Form 21B from Nathan's grasp. Nathan grabbed at it but missed, and Fulcher quickly pocketed it.

"I've got you at last," Fulcher said cheerily.

Nathan bowed his head in an admission of defeat. "You did indeed," Nathan said. "I should have known better. Did you teleport Travis first-"

"Deliberately, yes," Fulcher said. "To separate you from him, so he couldn't get in the way like he did last time. This has all been my setup. I knew you would come to the travel agency to escape the city, so I took the liberty of taking the place over. I think you'll agree, my plan was most efficacious."

"Very ingenious," Nathan agreed. "It must have taken a lot of planning."

"It took a certain amount of strategy, yes," Fulcher said calmly. "But now that I have your 21B, your papers are in order - more or less. There will be no more resurrection for you, Mr. Haynes. The next time you die, it will be the end of you, and you'll have to stay in the afterlife, just like everyone else. But as a courtesy, just to demonstrate that you were a worthy opponent, the next time you die, I will process your file myself. Professional courtesy, from one gentleman to another."

"Thank you," Nathan said. "That means a lot to me."

Behind them, the door opened and Brian slumped into the room.

"I'm very disappointed in you, Mr. Dithershoes," Director Fulcher said. "You haven't made any substantive action towards obtaining Mr. Haynes' signature at all. In the end I had to do everything myself. So I am afraid-"

Brian cringed. "-no! Not that!"

"-you'll have to continue on as Brian!"

Like a wounded wolf, Brian let out a soul-wrenching scream of despair, but Fulcher was not swayed. A second form appeared in Fulcher's hand, which he signed, and then he disappeared into thin air, with Nathan's 21B in his pocket.

So Nathan was left with Brian in the cold, dark, lonely room.

Chapter 29

Brian was hammering half-heartedly on Nathan's chest between his tears.

"This - is - all - your - fault," he stammered.

"I don't really see how you can think it's my fault," Nathan shot back. "I mean, if it hadn't been for me you never would have gotten the opportunity to change names in the first place. What's so bad about your name anyway? I think Brian-"

Brian wailed horribly. Between his sobs he was filling out a Form 88059 - Request For Authorization To Wallow In Despair, a Form 719438 - Authorization To Focus Abject Hatred On Another Human Being, and a Form 683732 - Notification Of The Start of a Vendetta.

Nathan patted him on the shoulder in consolation for a while, then decided he had better things to do than console bureaucrats and walked away. The travel agent and the security guard were gone from the lobby. Nathan supposed they had both been bureaucrats in disguise as well, or else acting on their behalf, and had deserted their posts since their task was fulfilled. He walked out into the cool of Dead Donkey's early evening, the scenic sunset in the distance complemented by the city's burning skyline. He sniffed the air, heavy with the musk of accelerants and raw sewage. He paused and listened to the distant melodious hum of the xylophone fences and the revolutionary yells of the Pluto Liberation Front, punctuated by the sounds of violent fighting and even more violent games of Muleball. He smiled to himself, because this was his home.

After lingering on the step of the travel agency for a minute or two, enjoying the ambiance, Nathan made his way back to his car, broke in, started the engine and drove back to his home.

A familiar pump-action shotgun sounded as he careened around the corner onto his block. The ensuing blast of buckshot knocked out one of his tires and sent metal shrapnel pinging in the vacant passenger compartment of his car.

"Whoops, sorry about that," Mr. Fletcher called out from his perch. "I was aiming for the streetlights."

Nathan looked around and saw most of the streetlights had been shot out. He sighed.

"Have you been shooting out the lights again?" he asked.

"They have been sneaking up on my property," Mr. Fletcher insisted, and took another shot at the streetlights.

Nathan took to the sidewalk, passed the huddled mess of wounded salesmen who had taken cover from Mr. Fletcher behind the fence, and approached his own door. He opened it and walked inside, kicked his shoes off, and started to whistle while he thought about doing his laundry. He went to the bathroom and washed some of the copious blood off of his hands, then realized he was quite hungry and went to the kitchen to make himself a sandwich. While he was getting the bread and mayo out, he looked out his window and saw his stack of corpses piled high in the backyard wheelbarrow and realized with a tinge of annoyance that he hadn't figured out what to do about them yet. After he put down his mayo knife, he resolved to call the morgue or the university or the pet shop or whoever he could interest in a pile of bones and picked up the phone receiver.

The line was dead.

Nathan quickly traced the cable with his finger and found it had been cut cleanly in two.

Just that moment, the lights came on in his living room. There, sitting in the greenest of Nathan's several green chairs, was the serial killer.

"Good evening," the serial killer said cheerily.

"Hello," Nathan responded pleasantly. "Would you like some sandwiches? I was just making them."

"You know, on balance I am feeling a little peckish. If it's not too much of an imposition..."

"Not at all," Nathan said, and made his serial killer a sandwich.

"Of course, I don't normally eat while I'm on the job," the serial killer continued. "It can cause problems with the authorities down the line."

"Ah," replied Nathan. "Bureaucracy. You don't need to tell me about bureaucracy. I've had about as much bureaucracy as I can handle today."

He handed his serial killer a plate with a sandwich on it. The serial killer accepted it and ate it gratefully.

"I'm famished," he explained as he wolfed it down.

"I am too," Nathan said. "I haven't had anything to eat all day except airplane food, a bagel, and a badger's whisker, and that was very accidental."

The serial killer licked his fingers clean, then crossed his legs and reclined himself into a slightly relaxed yet still very business-like position.

"Now, I felt that we ought to have a little chat. I've killed you twice now, but you're not dead."

"I'm not," confirmed Nathan.

"I wanted to ask you: why is that, exactly? Why do you keep coming back to life?"

And with that, Nathan launched into his lengthy story, which involved Brian and Ian and Donna and Director Fulcher and Travis and much more arson than Nathan had realized was oing on at the time, but memories are like that. Nathan xplained that his papers had not been in order so Director ulcher kept restoring him to a life as a matter of necessity.

The serial killer listened patiently to all this and then, inally, nodded in understanding.

"So it was all an administrative mix up. I should have nown it was something like that. If there's one thing that can e relied on to get in the way in life, it's bureaucracy." He ighed. "Well, fortunately, it's all worked itself out. I suppose nat we can put this behind us now that you've signed your 21B nd put your papers in order. Now you can die and stay dead - inless they have some other important form for you to sign vhen you die."

"I don't think so. Director Fulcher seemed very happy vhen he vanished off into nothing."

"Good, good. Then I can kill you. I know I've told you this ll before but it's extremely important that I kill you. If word got around that I tried to kill you but you'd come back to life - vhy - my reputation would be ruined. I regret it a little bit, Nathan, but it's all part of the job."

"I understand."

The serial killer took out his silenced pistol and flipped off he safety.

"Before you kill me, can I ask you a question?"

"Certainly," the serial killer answered. "Since you've been so civil with me... not many people are civil with serial killers. t's all boos and jeers and screams of terror. I don't like it. It gets very depressing after a while."

"I imagine it would."

"What was your question?"

"How did you become a serial killer?"

The serial killer told him. It was a much more complete answer than the serial killer had given than when Nathan had asked him just before his first murder. It was a tale of sadness and woe, but ultimately personal triumph.

The serial killer was living his dream. He had always wanted to do what he did now, ever since he was a little serial killer. He'd had a difficult childhood. His father had beaten him - beaten him at checkers, so the serial killer had killed him. After that life had gotten very hard for him, and he'd been shuttled from foster family to foster family, each of whom died in a series of mysterious and unrelated bloody knife accidents. Then the serial killer had grown up a little bit and gone to college, where he had studied criminology and medical psychology and taken a personality test that said he was perfectly suited to serial killer work, so he'd decided to give it a try for real. He'd started serial killing professionally (instead of his previous hobbyist work) in the streets of Dead Donkey as a relatively young man, where he'd had to compete with the Muleball Players' Association and the Confederation of Street Thugs for the attention of the local and international news media. Fortunately, he had eventually been able to overcome them by killing them, in a very scrappy, come-from-behind underdog win kind of a way. After he'd disposed of the MPA and the CST, wiping out a good chunk of the Dead Donkey Drug Dealers' and Pimps' Organization while he was at it, he had started to gain local fame for his many serial killing exploits. He considered his crowning achievement and the peak of his fame to be his successful execution of the Regio Boulevard parking attendant, who had long been considered by Dead Donkey serial killers to be the trickiest kill in the whole city. The parking attendant had sent him a posthumous letter of congratulations for his substantial skill at random assassination. From there it had all seemed like it was looking up, but the international news media just hadn't been that impressed. His kill rate, in terms of raw people, just wasn't competitive with some of the other nationally acknowledged serial killers - household names like the Parksfield Pulverizer and the Bagtown Liquidator, the latter of whom had once killed the entire population of Montana with nothing but an uncapped pen. So, the serial killer had to conduct more and more random killings in order to get his name out there, and to that end he had come to Nathan's house earlier that afternoon with a silenced pistol in his hand and a dream in his heart.

"That was very moving," Nathan said, after the serial killer had finished his story. "I hope you're able to kill lots and lots of people in the future," he said.

"Me too," the serial killer said emphatically as he checked his silencer. "I just know I'll make the FBI Most Wanted list one of these days."

"I have one more question though."

"Shoot. Not literally, of course. I'm the one doing the shooting here."

"When I was with my acquaintance, Travis Habsworth, he said that he thought there was some sort of intelligence behind your murdering me. A plot or scheme of some kind. Do you know anything about that?"

The serial killer shook his head.

"I'm sorry, but I'm a freelancer. I don't have any plot or scheme except killing the people in front of me." He gave a jolly smile.

"Ah, so it's just coincidence then?"

"Yes, just coincidence."

"You see, I ask because you somehow knew I came back to life after the first time. Do you remember?"

The serial killer frowned. "Yes... I heard about it through a colleague of mine." He shrugged and his frown disappeared. "Never mind that now. It's not important. I'm just going to go ahead and kill you so I can get home. I have a long commute."

He checked his silencer one last time and pressed the barrel of his pistol to Nathan's head.

There was a gunshot, but this time Nathan's world did not go black. Nathan felt the gun slip away from his temple and turned to see the serial killer slump down to the ground, dead.

Chapter 30

Nathan sat back in one of the less green of his several green chairs, stunned. He hadn't been expecting that.

A man Nathan had never seen before emerged from the shadows of Nathan's hallway. This man was tall with orderly brown hair and sunken eyes. He wore a sweeping kind of a robe.

"Hello, Nathan," the man said. He sat down in the greenest chair that the serial killer had only just recently vacated.

"You killed him," Nathan said, outraged. "He was my serial killer. I liked him! And you killed him!"

"I did," the robed man confirmed. "But it was necessary. He was about to kill you."

"I don't mind being killed, but it wasn't necessary to kill him," Nathan retorted.

"Ah, but it is quite necessary to my plans that you survive. You will not be nearly so useful to me dead as alive."

"What do you mean?" Nathan demanded. "Who are you?"

"I am Quaestor Dominique Delroy."

He paused dramatically. Nathan stared at him blankly. He had no idea who Quaestor Dominique Delroy was supposed to be.

"The Archdiogenian," elaborated Delroy. "The Grand Interlocutor."

Nathan continued to stare at him blankly.

"The Conmystic Logos," Delroy said insistently. "The Specifist's Designated One."

"Do you run a clothing store?" Nathan guessed tentatively.

"I'm head of the Church of Particularly Cynical Atheists," Delroy informed Nathan, looking a bit miffed that he'd had to spell it out. "I'm the most powerful atheist in Dead Donkey."

This was saying something. Nathan sat up a little. His mind cast around for something to say to a man of position and authority in his home.

"Can I offer you a sandwich?" he said at length.

"No thank you," the Conmystic Logos replied. "I came to fetch you."

"Why?"

"I am the person you asked our dead friend about." He kicked the serial killer with his foot. "I told him that you could be found here, and when you came back to life I told him about that too. It was necessary for my plans. The serial killer was just a cog in the works - an unknowing tool to be used by greater men."

Nathan assumed that Delroy was going to tell him what plan he was talking about, so Nathan sat quietly and thought about the cereal jingle again.

As expected, the Designated One began to explain zealously.

"I've long since realized that the universe must be run by bureaucrats. After all, if there is no god, there has to be someone running this whole universe, and if it's not god, it's got to be bureaucrats. That's only common sense. But not everyone sees it that way. Some very foolish people persist in believing that god exists and that life has meaning. I aim to change all that, but in order to convince the holdouts, I needed someone who could go to see for themselves what it was like on the other side - beyond the pale - in the world of death, where the bureaucrats live. Unfortunately, it's very difficult to find someone like that, because once you die, you're dead and you can't talk to anyone... but, if I could find someone whose papers were not in order, then I could use him. He would die and witness what lies beyond, then be sent back to life by the bureaucrats and tell us about it. We searched far and wide for such a person, and we finally came across you."

"How did you find me?" Nathan asked.

"We Particularly Cynical Atheists have infiltrated all levels of government and administration and worked tirelessly trying to find someone who had never signed any contracts that could compromise his position with the cosmic bureaucrats. Dr. Vegatillius is, of course, a Particularly Cynical Atheist. That is why he never made you sign anything. It's also the reason that he secured your body the second-to-last time that you died. Your bodies were very important for this. No one will believe a man with half his brain missing who says he's died and come back. But with your bodies - your bodies are proof! There are two here and my agents have already collected the other two. They stand as definitive evidence that you have died repeatedly and come back to life, and are therefore qualified to speak about what lies beyond the pale curtain of death. You can tell everyone about the bureaucracy. Then my congregation will grow. We'll be able to overcome the Atheist Absolutists, not to mention the United Atheist Confessionals and the Alliance of Messianic Atheists."

"The who?"

"The Alliance of Messianic Atheists. They believe there is no god and that one day a messiah will appear to tell everyone about it," he said off-handedly. "Maybe they're right. It could be you. Now, come with me."

He beckoned Nathan.

Nathan shook his head.

"I don't think I really want to come with you. You just

killed my only friend and murderer, so I'm not sure you're a very nice person to help."

"You don't really have a choice in the matter," the Archdiogenian said, and suddenly the room was full with the robed figures of Particularly Cynical Atheist zealots. They advanced on Nathan in that specially menacing way that only robed zealots can.

"You're going to tell everyone everything you know," Delroy continued. "And then no one will believe there is a god!"

"Why's that exactly?" Nathan asked warmly. "Just because there are bureaucrats in the afterlife doesn't mean there's no god."

"What?" Delroy said, momentarily taken aback. "Of course it does. It means the bureaucrats are running everything, not god. So therefore there is no god."

"No it doesn't," Nathan disagreed, shaking his head. "That's like saying that there's no President because bureaucrats run the United States. The bureaucrats in the afterlife are enforcing rules, but who set the rules? God, probably."

Delroy furrowed his brow.

"And what's more," Nathan went on, "there are bureaucrats in the Bible. St. Peter's supposed to stand at the gates of heaven and judge whether you're allowed in or not, right? What is that if it isn't bureaucracy? St. Peter's a bureaucrat. He's even usually shown having a line of people waiting in paintings. Maybe," Nathan continued thoughtfully, "Director Fulcher is St. Peter."

This seemed deeply unlikely to him, but after everything he'd gone through this afternoon, he had to admit that anything was possible.

"Besides, I never saw past the bureaucracy," Nathan said. "Maybe if I'd signed the 21B in the first place I'd have gone to heaven. Who knows? I don't."

There was a long silence.

"Blast," the Grand Interlocutor said, his brow furrowed. "We'll just have to kill you."

"You can kill me if you like-" Nathan started, and that was as far as he got, because Delroy took this as permission and shot him in the head.

His last thought before he died was that he was starting to see Travis' point about Dead Donkey being a very violent city.

Chapter 31

"Station Number Four, please."

Nathan found himself standing back in front of the frumpy woman, her familiar look of disdain boring holes through his chest.

"Hello," he said happily. "Good to see you again."

The frumpy woman just glared at him for a while, then pointed to the door that had materialized nearby.

"I'll go see Director Fulcher then," Nathan pressed on. "Bye."

He stepped out into the hallway, deciding that the frumpy woman was a hard person to know. Nathan crossed to the door he knew to be Director Fulcher's and knocked.

"Come in," Fulcher's imperious voice boomed.

Nathan entered.

Fulcher looked up at Nathan and gave him an extremely wry smile.

"Ah, I wasn't expecting you quite so soon, Mr. Haynes, though I suppose this isn't too much out of line with your previous arrivals. How did you come to be with us this time?"

"I was murdered by robed atheists who were scared I would tell people there was a god," Nathan said perfunctorily, and sat down in his chair.

Fulcher folded his hands.

"Normally there is a special form for that but in your case your first death takes precedence," Fulcher said. "Now, let's finish putting your papers in order and get you processed, shall we?"

"Okay," Nathan agreed.

Fulcher reached into his desk and produced Nathan's

impossibly large file, which he slammed down on his desk (which had itself suddenly grown to inconceivably accommodating proportions).

"Before we get started, I'd just like to ask one last thing," Nathan said.

"Certainly," Fulcher answered magnanimously, his face breaking into a smirk.

"Last time we spoke, you started telling me something about the universe and how I fit into everything, but then you stopped and said you couldn't tell me any more until my forms were signed. Now that they're signed, do you think you could tell me?"

"Of course," Fulcher said with a grin. "Where was I? Right. The start of the universe. Well, it was manageable at first, but the problem with the universe is that so very many things happen on a day to day basis. In fact, nearly everything is doing a huge number of things at once. Think about it - particles bumping into each other, neutrinos decaying into other kinds of neutrinos, objects influencing each other with their gravity... every single one of those things requires a form. The number of forms grew exponentially, and soon we had a backlog of more than a quizillion forms to file. Time was getting very dilated - not like the beginning when it moved fast - and even though we'd expanded the universe so things wouldn't bump into each other as often, we just didn't have the manpower to comply with our statutory obligations vis-a-vis the basic forces of the universe. So we hatched a very long term plan. We found a suitable planet with a long-lived main-line sun that was a reasonable temperature and didn't have any nearby gamma ray bursts or anything, and we assembled some self-replicating goop out of primordial acids and lipids. It was a bit of a liberty under our assigned powers, I admit, but it was much better than simply defaulting on our legal obligations."

Nathan frowned. He was trying to understand.

"Are you saying you created life on Earth?"

Fulcher nodded.

"Exactly. And just a few billion years later, humans had evolved. Everything went just as we'd planned. Humans developed language and culture and finally - politics - government - and inevitably-"

"Bureaucracy," Nathan finished.

"Yes. You're catching on. So we gave them souls so they could come here when they died, and we could recruit them as bureaucrats to help us run reality. And that's what keeps reality running at the smooth, regular pace and extremely high resolution that you've come to expect."

"You're trying to tell me," Nathan said slowly, "that the meaning of life-"

"Is bureaucracy," Director Fulcher said with a nod. "Of course. How else is reality supposed to keep on going? Why, if it weren't for us, it would be chaos out there. Totally unstructured chaos. Dogs would be mewing and buildings would be doing backflips and the sun would be a dark and purple square. Someone has to impose order."

"I don't think I want to be a bureaucrat for the rest of eternity," Nathan said.

"Are you sure? The benefits are very good. And you get one weekend off per quizillion years."

"I'm sure."

"Oh well, to be honest we probably wouldn't have wanted you as a bureaucrat anyway. You're a bit too unpredictable. Not to mention that you're obviously no fan of paperwork." He

hrugged. "So we'll just get you processed and moved on, shall
we?"

"I don't want to be processed. I think I'd rather go back to
fe."

Director Fulcher leaned across the table with a patronizing
mile on his face.

"My dear Mr. Haynes, now that you've signed your 21B,
ou don't have a choice. You're going to be processed and
noved on regardless."

Nathan did not smile back.

Fulcher's smile widened, though, and he leaned back
nanagerially and opened Nathan's file.

"Is that my 21B on the top?" Nathan asked, peering at it.

"Yes it is," Fulcher confirmed.

"Maybe you ought to take a closer look at that."

"Take a closer look at what exac-" Fulcher looked at the
21B and did a double-take. He stared at it, then gawked in
lisbelief.

"I'm getting very fed up with everyone thinking that just
because I'm missing part of my brain I'm stupid," Nathan said.
"It's very insulting."

"It's not signed," Fulcher said, staring at the 21B. "But you
signed it. I signed it. I brought it here."

He stared wildly at Nathan.

"Did you do this?" he demanded.

"Yes. I knew after you sent Donna and Ian and Brian after
me and they all failed that you'd eventually come yourself, and
while I was walking around with Travis in Dead Donkey, I
found a piece of transparent plastic and picked it up. This piece
of transparent plastic," Nathan added, producing it from his
pocket. "When we went into the travel agency and then saw the

supervisor there, I knew immediately that it was you. I recognized you because I'd seen you so many times, and when you asked me to sign the form I knew it must be a 21B. I asked you a question about the machine so you'd turn your head away for a second, and then when you did I slipped this piece of plastic over the 21B, which is the thing I signed. It was dark and shadowy where I was standing so you didn't notice. You never got my signature."

Fulcher gritted his teeth in annoyance. His face went red and he was breathing hard. His fists clenched.

"Clever of you," he said after a while. "This doesn't change anything. I'll be after you-"

"You signed it too," Nathan said.

Fulcher's face suddenly went from red to white.

"What?" he said, his voice barely a whisper.

"You signed it too," Nathan repeated. "I knew that you would have to sign it when you came because the frumpy woman at Station Four told me that the 21B needed a countersignature, so I knew you would have to countersign, so you also signed the piece of plastic. We both signed it. When I grabbed at you I wasn't trying to get the 21B back. I wanted the piece of plastic, which I got. It wasn't blank when you signed it. I wrote a contract on it. Would you like to hear what it says?"

If Nathan had been pressed to describe Fulcher at that moment, he would have called him white as an albino ghost with lyme disease. Nathan took out the plastic sheet and unfurled it onto the desk. Letters in black marker were barely visible on the transparent surface.

Fulcher stared at it.

"What does it say?" he whispered.

"Oh, nothing too important," Nathan replied. "It just says that you and all the other bureaucrats will stop trying to get me to sign a 21B or any other form, and any of your forms I sign in the past or the future are null and void, and you will stop bothering me. Oh, and it says no one will ever be able to steal my house by tricking me into signing anything either. That's pretty much it."

Fulcher babbled.

"B-but that means?"

"I win," Nathan said cheerily. "I told you we should have played Monopoly. I'm not very good at that, so you might have won."

For a full minute, Fulcher sat there ashen faced while the cereal jingle played in Nathan's head two or three times. At last, Fulcher shook his head in disbelief.

"Then I have no choice," he said finally. "I have to send you back. I admit defeat. You win, Mr. Haynes."

He held out his hand. Nathan gallantly shook it.

Then with a weary sigh, Fulcher reached into his desk and took out a form, which Nathan recognized as the form that sent him back to the regular world.

Just before he signed it, Fulcher paused and looked Nathan in the eye.

"I take back what I said before, Mr. Haynes. You would have made a splendid bureaucrat."

Nathan felt rather flattered.

Then Fulcher signed the form, and Nathan began to dissolve back into reality.

Chapter 32

Nathan found himself back in his own living room. To his great surprise, the cynical atheists had gone, leaving only their robes behind, and Travis was in their place.

"Travis!" Nathan said in shock. "I thought you went to Albany."

"One of the tricks to teleportation is not to observe yourself until you're where you want to go," Travis replied. "I waited until I was back in Dead Donkey, but by then you'd already gone. I assumed you went back to your house, so I came here... but it was too late. You were already dead."

"But what happened to the Particularly Cynical Atheists?" Nathan asked, looking at the robes.

"Oh. I convinced them they did not exist." Travis smiled. "I'm good at that sort of thing. I'm much more surprised to see you, though. I thought I was too late. After Director Fulcher tricked you, you should have stayed dead. What happened?"

Nathan explained everything. By the end, Travis was smiling.

"So you are the only man alive other than myself who can claim to be truly free of bureaucracy," he said. "You are free from death and all the other contractual and legal obligations that normally bind people. You are effectively immortal and in some respects all powerful. What are you going to do now?"

Nathan thought about this for a moment and came to a swift conclusion.

"I'm going to do my laundry," he said, and disappeared down the hallway.

(Finis.)

Message to the Reader

Dear reader,

Thank you very much for taking a chance on an independent author. You Are Dead. (Sign Here Please) represents yet another format experiment for me. It's the first pure comedy novel that I've ever written, and I hope you enjoyed reading it as much as I did writing it.

If you liked You Are Dead. (Sign Here Please), I'd very much appreciate it if you rated and reviewed this book or shared it with your friends. I rely on writing for my income, and I have struggled to get the word out about my novels, and just a little help from you could mean worlds to me. Since reviews are my only potential source of feedback, I also find them invaluable for my future writing.

I have written a large number of other books, some comedic, some serious. They are all available on Amazon and other online retail outlets, and you can find them by searching my name.

Best,
--Andrew Stanek

PS: If you want to join my mailing list, go to http://eepurl.com/bhTc9H. I send out notices about my writing and sometimes give out good stuff, like free books and advance copies of my new novels to people on the list. I won't send you spam. You can contact me at StanekBooks@gmail.com if you just want to talk to me about something.

(The cosmic bureaucrats are statutorily obligated to notify you that this page was left intentionally blank. If you are reading this message you must therefore fill out Form 599298-Q: Acknowledgement of Bureaucratic Creation of Blank Page Notification-Related Paradox.)

Printed in Great Britain
by Amazon

87280314R00123